Caven is on the run. He was imprisoned for a good reason. But he has no intention of living behind bars for the rest of his life. So as soon as he had the chance, he left the Ogorth clan behind and headed for the human world.

But things there are more complicated than he expected. Sebastian's life is perfectly normal until he stumbles on a murder. He runs, but when the murderer finds him, he thinks he's going to die, too.

And he almost does.

Even though Caven knows he shouldn't get involved, he helps the human escape. He's been yearning for home, and keeping Sebastian safe is as good an excuse as any other to go back to the clan and beg for their forgiveness. Even if Caven is stuck in a cell, at least he'll be home.

What Caven doesn't expect is to fall for Sebastian — or to get pregnant. It's the first step for the queen to realize there was more to his betrayal than she knew and that he's not the enemy he tried to be.

But with Caven's father disgusted by what Caven has done, Sebastian's family being possibly in danger, and the meeting with the government representative approaching, Caven and Sebastian are both entirely lost — and so very different. Can they make things work between them and raise the second human-dragon hybrid of the clan while also keeping the clan, Sebastian, and his family safe? Or is it too much for their shoulders?

Turquoise Revelation
Copyright © 2022 Catherine Lievens
ISBN: 978-1-4874-3639-1
Cover art by Angela Waters

Published by eXtasy Books Inc

Look for us online at:
www.eXtasybooks.com

Turquoise Revelation
Ogorth Clan 6

By

Catherine Lievens

CHAPTER ONE

No one noticed when Caven slipped away. He'd done it on purpose, knowing the fight with the humans would distract the others. He'd hoped it would be enough for him to be able to leave without them noticing, and he was right. Now he was free, albeit on the run.

It was terrifying.

He stayed in his human form as he made his way through the forest. He'd never been on his own. He'd never *not* had a home. He'd planned on leaving so he wouldn't have to return to his cell once they were back at the palace, but now that he had, he didn't know what to do.

He clearly should have planned this better.

He could still hear the sounds of dragons and humans fighting somewhere behind him, but he knew the queen was safe, which was all that mattered. Her inner circle would make sure nothing happened to her. They were tight-knit and the backbone of the queen's presence on the throne. Still, Caven felt slightly guilty at the thought that he could have done more to help the clan. He should be defending the clan and Queen Ita from the humans, not running away.

But there was no going back for him.

There wasn't much to do for a dragon who didn't have a clan, which was what Caven was now. He could find another one, but he doubted anyone would welcome him. He didn't want anything to do with the clans who would, because they were traitors of the worst kind, and that wasn't someone Caven wished to ally himself with. They'd demand he betray the Ogorth clan, which Caven would never do.

That only left one possibility. No matter how much he didn't like it, he'd have to blend in with humans.

Caven looked down at himself. Even though he was in his human form, there was little human about him. A glance would be enough for anyone to know he didn't belong, and with humans now aware that dragons could turn into a human form, it could spell trouble for him. So, staying with humans was out, too. What did that leave?

He supposed he could stay in the forest. If he did it right, he could hide in the trees while also being close enough to a human town that he'd be able to get food and whatever else he needed. They wouldn't even have to see him. He could sneak in and out of town during the night when humans slept. Anything would be better than going back to the cell he'd been stuck in since his cousin had arrested him.

He stumbled on a root at the thought of his cousin. He wasn't innocent in this situation, and was very much aware of it. He'd been trying to protect the clan in the only way he knew how to, and he'd been an idiot. He should have known better than to go after the people who were important to the queen, but it had been easy, or at least, it had felt like it would be. He shouldn't have listened to his father, but then that went for every single situation Caven had found himself in. He now knew that taking Ita's place on the throne wouldn't have saved the clan, no matter how many times his father had told him it would.

He swallowed and pushed past a branch. He let it go too quickly, and it slapped him in the face, scratching him. He scowled at the tree, but he continued walking.

He wasn't used to any of this. This forest wasn't his place. The cell he'd been in wasn't his place. His place was at the palace, surrounded by his allies. His place was on the throne in his cousin's position, according to his father.

Caven wasn't sure about that anymore.

He'd allowed his father to convince him that everything would be okay once he was king. He'd allowed his father to convince him that he *wanted* to be king and that being king would make him happy. Caven now knew that wasn't true. He'd watched the queen long enough to know how hard her job was. It would probably be an easier job with him not there to be an asshole, but he couldn't help but worry.

Without him there to keep his father at bay while also smoothing things out with some of the other clans his father had allied himself with, would the queen be able to keep the clan safe?

The Ogorth clan was Caven's entire life. He'd been doing his best to keep it safe, which hadn't been easy when his father was actively working against both the clan and the queen. Caven had been stupid enough to go along with what his father wanted because he thought it was what he should do, but he knew better now. The problem was that his cousin didn't. The queen wasn't aware that Caven's father had been involved in all of this and that he was probably behind the fact that the humans had found them. Caven wouldn't put it past him to have told the humans where they could find dragons in the hopes they'd capture Ita and some of her allies.

Humans were greedy, and even though they now knew that dragons could turn into humans, Caven wasn't surprised they still hunted them. They were afraid of what they didn't know, and they didn't know dragons. It was entirely their fault, too. They'd been hunting dragons for hundreds of years, so who would blame dragons for hiding?

But Caven supposed he would have to get used to being around humans. He'd have to be careful, because he'd end up killed and torn apart if he wasn't. There was no going back to the Ogorth clan, though. After what Caven had done, there was no place for him there.

He tried to ignore the pang of sadness and pain in his chest. He'd done what he'd done, and it was too late to change his actions. It was too late for him to work with his cousin rather than against her, too late to fix what he'd broken. This was his life now, and he needed to get used to it.

As he stumbled on another root, he couldn't help but wonder if he'd succeed and what the next days, weeks, and months would look like for him.

Sebastian grabbed the bottle of milk and closed the fridge door. He hummed along with the music coming from somewhere above his head, wondering who had chosen it. Was it the grocery store owner? It didn't look like something the kid at the till would pick, but what did Sebastian know? Considering how late it was—just past midnight—the kid couldn't be as young as he looked. Either that, or his parents didn't care that he worked the night shift at the grocery store.

Sebastian carried the milk to the checkout kid, waited for him to take his money, then left, still humming. It would take a while to get the song out of his mind, which meant it would drive him nuts for the next few days. He supposed it could have been worse, and he whistled as he headed back home. Now that he had milk for his breakfast, he could finally go to bed.

He was still humming as he walked past the entrance of an alley. The area wasn't dangerous per se, but sometimes he crossed paths with people he'd rather not meet in a dark alley. That was why he wasn't surprised when he heard someone calling for help deeper in the alley. His first instinct was to rush there and help, but that could land him in more trouble than he wanted. It wasn't unheard of for people to get stabbed and killed in this area, which was why his father always said that Sebastian needed to move. Sebastian agreed, but his father wasn't the one paying his rent. He'd have known Sebastian couldn't afford anything better if he had been.

"Help!" the woman called out again.

Her voice was softer this time, and Sebastian could hear the sound of flesh hitting flesh. It made him cringe, and even though he might be putting himself in danger, he couldn't just stay back and let the woman be hurt. He rushed into the alley, praying he wouldn't regret it.

He was careful as he moved as quickly as possible. The woman was whimpering now, which at least meant she was still alive. Sebastian wouldn't forgive himself if she died and he could have stepped in sooner.

The alley was dark, but one of the businesses had a light over its back door. That meant that Sebastian could see what was happening ahead of him, and it made his stomach churn and his mouth taste like blood.

A man was standing with his back to him. Sebastian couldn't see the man's face, but he could see the woman he was holding by the throat. When the man raised his free hand again, she screwed her eyes shut as if she didn't want to see the fist coming toward her. Her lower lip was already bleeding, and both her eyes were swelling up.

Sebastian opened his mouth to tell the man to stop, but the man hit her before he could. Sebastian sucked in a breath, and while the punch was not enough to get him to stop moving, the gun the man took out was.

Shit. Sebastian wanted to help this woman, but he didn't want to die, and he suspected that if he tried anything, that was what would happen. It wouldn't take much for this guy to turn his gun on Sebastian instead of her and shoot him. He'd probably shoot both of them.

Sebastian stepped behind a dumpster, feeling like a coward but knowing he wasn't. He pressed himself as far back as he could, pushing his body into the tiny space between the wall and the dumpster. He screwed his eyes shut, biting down on his lower lip when he heard the shot. He bit down so hard that he could taste blood, but he stayed where he was, as silent as possible, ignoring the stench and what had just happened. His instincts told him to run back from where he'd come from, but the guy who'd just shot the woman would see and hear him. Then he'd probably shoot Sebastian, too, and it wasn't something Sebastian wanted to consider.

No, he'd better stay where he was.

The sound of something heavy hitting the ground almost made him whimper. He bit harder on his lip, not caring that he was hurting himself. It was either this or death, so it was an easy choice. He heard the man move, then footsteps coming closer. He held his breath, praying the man hadn't noticed him. He'd been busy hurting the woman, so there was a good chance he hadn't, but Sebastian couldn't breathe as the man walked past the dumpster.

As he did so, he stepped under the light shining from above the back door. It illuminated his face, and Sebastian recognized him.

Everyone knew him in the neighborhood. Some said he had links to the mafia, others that he was a serial killer. Sebastian didn't know which of those was true or if either was, but he did know that Patrick O'Neill was dangerous. He'd known that before he'd seen the guy shoot a woman, so it wasn't like he had needed any proof. He terrorized the neighborhood, dealt drugs, and hurt people, but Sebastian had never crossed paths with him so far, and Patrick didn't know him. He didn't have a reason to hurt Sebastian.

He definitely would if he found out Sebastian had seen him kill someone.

Sebastian must have made a movement, something he wasn't aware of, and it got Patrick's attention. His eyes narrowed, and he turned his head, his gaze stopping on

Sebastian. Sebastian held his breath, hoping the darkness behind the dumpster would hide him, but he wasn't too sure about that anymore.

Then something made a noise behind Patrick. He jerked in that direction, raising one of his hands, and Sebastian saw the gun in it.

What was he supposed to do? He was pretty sure Patrick had realized someone was hiding behind the dumpster, which meant he was about to kill Sebastian. As tempting as it was to cower here and pray that wouldn't be the case, Sebastian couldn't.

Without overthinking it so he wouldn't freak out, he threw himself away from the dumpster and toward the alley entrance. Patrick had stepped back, and Sebastian didn't stick around to see what he did. He didn't have to, anyway, because the next thing he knew, something whizzed past his ear.

Patrick was shooting at him.

Sebastian ran faster, even though he was already out of breath and his calves burned. He didn't stop running, even when he hit the entrance of the alley. He couldn't afford to with Patrick right behind him. He could hear him coming after him.

So Sebastian ran. He ran back toward his apartment building, praying Patrick wasn't behind him. He didn't think so, because he couldn't hear anyone following him, which had to be a good thing.

He didn't dare slow down enough to check.

He didn't stop running even when he reached his building. Instead of waiting for the elevator, he ran up the stairs. His legs felt like jelly and his lungs were burning, but he managed to get to his door. His hand trembled as he pushed the key into the lock, and when he finally managed to open the door, he threw himself into the apartment and slammed it behind himself.

He was still clutching the bottle of milk.

"What the fuck happened to you?" his cousin asked from the couch.

After putting down the milk, Sebastian pressed his hands against his knees and faced Christian. "I saw something," he said, panting.

Christian rose into a sitting position, but he didn't let go of the remote control. "What? Because it kind of looks like you've seen a ghost."

Sebastian shook his head. "Not a ghost. Patrick O'Neill killing a woman."

Christian gaped, and the remote fell from his fingers. "Are you fucking with me?"

"I wouldn't do that, not about something like this. I heard a noise in an alley, and I wanted to help the woman, so I went there. He had a gun, and he shot her after beating her."

Christian stared. "Did he see you?"

Sebastian nodded. "I hid, but he saw me, and I had to run away. He shot at me, but he didn't get me."

"Does he know who you are?"

"I have no idea." And the thought that Patrick O'Neill might be able to recognize Sebastian was terrifying. He hadn't followed Sebastian home tonight, but what about tomorrow? Would he be able to find him? Would he kill Sebastian?

And if he didn't, what would Sebastian do about all of this?

CHAPTER TWO

Caven missed his cell at the palace. That was how bad things were going for him.

He glared at the rat on the other side of the empty room, and the rat glared back. If Caven hadn't been a dragon shifter, he'd have run away screaming. As it was, he bared his teeth, and the rat scampered away.

Caven looked around. He'd known meeting rats was a possibility when he'd chosen this place to spend the night, but that didn't mean he enjoyed it.

He didn't enjoy anything about his new life away from the palace. He was hungry and dirty, and he wanted to go home. The only reason he hadn't run back as fast as he could was that he wasn't sure he'd be welcome. If they limited themselves to sticking him back into his cell, he wouldn't care. He wouldn't put it past his cousin's inner circle to demand his head on a silver platter, though, and he couldn't risk it.

So, rats it was. He'd have to get used to having that kind of roommate.

His stomach growled, and he got to his feet. He'd stayed in his human form since he'd arrived at the edge of whatever town he was in, even though it would be obvious to anyone who saw him that he was a dragon shifter. He didn't look human, even when he stood on two legs. But staying in this form made it easier for him to hide, and not only that. He wouldn't be able to find food if he shifted into his dragon form.

He'd been sneaking around this area of town, stealing food when he found it. It wasn't enough, but he didn't know what else to do. He hadn't been prepared for any of this, and it scared him. He'd thought it would be fairly easy for him to survive, but he wasn't too sure of that anymore. What if he couldn't find enough food? And even if he did, what was his end goal? He couldn't continue living in this abandoned building. He didn't want to, but where else could he go? The palace was out, as was any other clan. So where did that leave Caven?

It left him in a spot where he missed his cell, for fuck's sake.

Maybe he could try going back. Maybe the queen would be lenient, since he'd helped her with the meetings and the other clans. She might even allow him to return to his old life, although he didn't hold that much hope.

But he was too proud. He knew he was in trouble and out of his depth, but he didn't want to admit that to anyone but himself. If he tried going back, Ita would demand an explanation of where he'd been and an apology. Caven couldn't do that. He couldn't make himself look weak, not even to the queen. Besides, no one back home trusted him. They'd probably think he'd betrayed the clan, and he couldn't even blame them for that. They didn't understand that everything he'd done, he'd done because he'd thought it was the right thing to do to keep the clan safe. If he weren't himself, he wouldn't believe his words, either.

The sound of wings flapping made him glare at the broken window. The pigeon sat just outside of it, staring at him.

That was something else Caven was learning to deal with. It wasn't enough that he had to share his living space with rats, but pigeons — or as he thought of them, as the rats of the sky — also came in. He had no way to shield this place from them or anything else.

He looked around. This wasn't his place, anyway. It wasn't his home, and he doubted it had been a home in a long time.

The room was empty. Everything that hadn't been nailed

to the floor had been taken away, leaving torn carpet and dirty walls. The broken windows meant plants and animals had come in, along with rain. The area around the window was covered in leaves and moisture, and the wall and floor were turning black.

He huffed and moved toward the door. Crying over what had happened to him and his situation wouldn't help. He was hungry, which meant he needed to find food. *That* was what he should focus on.

He wasn't going home, so he needed to stop thinking that he would. This was his new life, and he should get used to it and make the most of what he had.

Which, at the moment, was nothing.

Sebastian looked around nervously. He expected Patrick O'Neill to jump out of every shadow and every dark corner, and he wished he could have avoided going to the store tonight. Unfortunately for him and Christian, the fridge was empty, which meant that someone needed to go to the grocery store if they wanted to eat. Sebastian had tried to convince Christian to go, but just as Christian had been about to leave, his boss had called, and he hadn't been able to avoid answering the phone.

So here Sebastian was, on his way to the grocery store, looking around as if he expected someone to jump him.

He did. He hadn't seen or heard from Patrick O'Neill since that evening a few days ago, but he had no doubt Patrick was looking for him. He prayed the man wouldn't find him, but knowing his luck, he'd have to face him eventually.

Sebastian had been keeping an eye out for any news about the woman in the alley. It had taken a little over a day, but eventually, someone had found her. His heart had broken for her as he'd watched the news and the anchorman explained what happened to her.

She'd been a college student. Apparently she'd been using drugs, and Patrick was her dealer. Sebastian didn't know what had happened between them to push Patrick to hit and kill her, but the news guy said that it was probably a drug deal gone wrong. Even if that was true, she hadn't deserved to die. Sebastian wished he'd done more for her, but if he'd tried, he would have been killed, too. That was what he reminded himself of when he woke up in the middle of the night, terrified and screaming, her image printed behind his eyelids.

He didn't know what to do. He didn't want Patrick to get away with killing that woman, but what would happen if he went to the cops? There was a reason Patrick O'Neill did everything he did in the neighborhood. The cops turned a blind eye, and no one would convince Sebastian that Patrick didn't have allies on the force. It would be too easy for one of the cops to betray him and give Patrick his name and address. Then Patrick would come, and he'd kill Sebastian.

It wasn't fair, but Sebastian supposed that life in general wasn't.

He jumped at the sound of a bottle rolling on the ground somewhere close. He looked around, trying to see what had happened, but he was alone. The night felt darker than it was, and he hurried toward the grocery store. He needed to get there, then go home. He had to stop freaking himself out and focus on what he was supposed to do, not on what might happen.

He reached the grocery store and was about to go in when the door opened. His eyes widened, and, instead of going forward, he rushed back and turned the corner around the store.

Apparently, Patrick O'Neill shopped in the same grocery store as Sebastian. Either that, or he'd somehow found out Sebastian came here and was trying to find him.

Before Sebastian could decide what to do, Patrick appeared. He had a satisfied expression, which told Sebastian he'd been looking for him. He was going to kill Sebastian, and while Sebastian doubted he'd be able to stop Patrick, he could at least make it hard for him.

Once again, he turned and ran.

This time, he could hear footsteps coming after him. Patrick wouldn't let him out of this easily, or at all if he managed. If Sebastian wanted a chance to make it, he needed to leave Patrick behind, but how was he supposed to do that? The streets were empty, and he couldn't exactly go around knocking on doors. No one in their right mind would open to him.

But there were plenty of abandoned buildings around. Maybe he could get to one and find a place to hide. He didn't want to lead Patrick home, just in case. If Patrick were to kill him, at least Christian would be okay. If Sebastian brought Patrick home, though, Christian might be in danger, and that was the last thing Sebastian wanted.

He ran down the street, knowing which abandoned building he wanted to sneak into. He tried the front door, but it was locked, and he panicked. He took his phone out of his pocket as he moved around the building, hoping he'd find an opening at the back. As he did so, he tried to dial nine-one-one, but there was no signal.

He was on his own.

There was a boarded-up door at the back of the building. Sebastian pushed his phone back into his pocket, looked behind himself, then tried to pry open the door. Someone had nailed it shut, but the nails had rusted, and he quickly managed to free one side of the wood.

"Gotcha," someone murmured behind Sebastian.

He screamed and turned. There was nowhere for him to go, but that didn't mean he didn't try to find a way to escape. He could have run away from Patrick, but he couldn't see anything in the darkness and had no way of knowing what he'd find if he did. Besides, Patrick was holding a gun.

Patrick stepped closer. "So you were the one spying on me the other night."

Sebastian swallowed. Patrick hadn't killed him yet, so maybe that wasn't what he was after? It had to be a good sign, right? "I don't know what you're talking about," he said in a shaking voice.

Patrick stepped closer. There was little to no light where they stood, but Sebastian didn't need to see the man to know what he looked like or what he was planning.

"Don't you?" Patrick asked. "Because I saw you the other night. You were hiding behind a dumpster."

"I was home."

"But the grocery store clerk said you bought milk."

How had Patrick known?

"That's how I tracked you down," Patrick explained. "I saw the milk when you ran away, and I went to the nearest grocery store. I asked the clerk about the guy who'd just bought milk, and he told me everything he knew about you, including that you shop there often, usually at this time of night. I've been waiting for you the past few days."

By now, Patrick was so close that Sebastian could smell he'd been drinking. He didn't know why, but for some reason, that surprised him. Considering their situation, he would have thought Patrick would want to be in his right mind. Still, maybe Sebastian could use this to his advantage. How much had Patrick drunk? Was he at least tipsy?

"So, you saw me kill that girl. What am I supposed to do with you?" Patrick asked.

He'd raised the gun, and Sebastian couldn't look away from it. He also couldn't stop imagining what it would feel like to be shot. Would it hurt? Of course it would. He didn't need to get shot to know that. Where would Patrick shoot him? Would he go for death right away, or would he want to make this last? He was clearly pissed that Sebastian had seen what he'd done, but maybe the alcohol would change things.

Or maybe it wouldn't. There was only one thing Sebastian could do, and while he didn't think it would work, it wouldn't stop him from trying.

He pressed his back harder against the wall. "Please," he begged. "I didn't see anything that night. I mean, I saw someone was beating up that girl and that they shot her, but I never saw the person's face."

"If you hadn't known it was me before, you do now. Begging me won't stop what's about to happen."

Since it wouldn't, Sebastian did the only other thing he could think of.

He screamed.

Caven had been about to leave the building when he heard the voices. There were two, both human and both male. They were at the back of the building from which he usually left through a window, which meant he was stuck. Since he was hungry, he decided to wait it out, and he hovered there, right beside the door one of the humans had tried to open.

Which was why he'd heard everything the humans were saying.

He shouldn't intervene. For one, he was a dragon, and the humans would probably freak out. Also, this was his safe place, his home. He couldn't put it in jeopardy for a human.

But what would happen if the bad human killed the other one? There would be cops, which was one more thing Caven wanted to avoid. If cops came around and started poking in the building, they'd find out he'd been living there.

He was startled when something heavy hit the wood that covered the door. There was a whimper, then the sound of smacking.

He had to do something.

He hesitated, looking around, but there was no way he could shift here. He'd hurt himself, and he wasn't as good at fighting in his human form. As a dragon, the sheer mass of his body was usually enough, especially against a human.

So, instead of climbing through the window, he ran up the stairs.

He'd been here long enough to know which steps he shouldn't walk on, and he skipped them on his way to the roof—including the one his leg had gone through the first time he'd put his weight onto it. He was slightly panting when he got there, but he could still hear the two humans downstairs when he listened. Clearly, the bad one was planning to take his time hurting the other one.

He was cruel, but no crueler than Caven had been, which made Caven's stomach churn. Had he been like this? Was this what the others saw when they looked at him? It was no wonder they'd locked him up and wanted nothing to do with him.

But he wasn't a bad person. He'd made wrong choices, but that didn't mean he had to do so now.

So he shifted.

It came to him as easily as breathing or drinking water. One second, he stood on two feet. The next, his four feet were on the roof, and he stretched out his long legs. He turned his head this way and that, opened his wings, and shook them.

The screaming from downstairs told him he was out of time and that if he was planning on saving the human, he needed to step in now.

He stepped to the edge of the roof. Something cracked under his weight, but he didn't pay it any attention. He threw himself off the roof, calculating how many seconds he'd be falling before he hit the ground. There wasn't much space behind the building, but he'd fit, even though it would be tight.

He landed behind the bad human. The one with his back pressed against the wall stared at Caven with wide eyes, and the one with the gun started turning around to check what he was watching. Before he could do something stupid like trying to shoot Caven, Caven grabbed him with one paw and flung him away. He winced at the sound of the human slamming against a wall. If he wasn't mistaken, he'd even heard the crack of a bone breaking.

He wasn't about to stick around and check. He didn't even care if the human was dead or alive, although from the whimpers coming from the direction in which he'd landed, he was alive.

Before anything else happened, Caven reached for the other human.

The man looked around frantically, no doubt for a place to escape. There was nowhere for him to go, though, and Caven could already hear the bad human getting to his feet.

He hadn't looked at that one, but he could easily see the one in front of him, even though it was dark. He had blond curls that tumbled over his forehead, almost long enough to hang in front of his eyes. His skin seemed pale, but it was dotted with darker spots Caven couldn't identify. Although shorter than Caven would be in his human form, the man was tall and slender. It was easy to grab him and push, jumping into the air.

The very edge of Caven's wings brushed against the buildings around them, but not enough to stop him. The human screamed. He sounded terrified, which Caven could understand. Between the fact that he'd been kidnapped by a dragon and the fact that someone had tried to kill him, he had to be terrified. Caven wanted to reassure him, but even more, he wanted to save him from the other human. The problem was that he didn't know how to do that. He didn't know how to do many things, and one of those things was how to save a human. He needed to take this human away, but where?

He headed for the roof, since he couldn't fly around without a destination. Even if the other human got back to his feet and followed them, it would take him a moment to reach the roof. Hopefully, that would be enough for Caven to shift and ask this human where he should take him. If it wasn't, well, Caven supposed he could fly for a few hours. That should be enough to leave the human with the gun behind.

Sebastian was still screaming. They landed on the roof, and as soon as the dragon let him go, he ran.

He didn't go far.

The dragon extended an arm and caught him, dragging him close. It pulled Sebastian up to its massive head and looked at him with a big, round eye.

Sebastian looked back. What could he do?

He had no idea what had just happened. Patrick O'Neill had been about to kill him, but this *dragon* had landed and thrown Patrick against the wall. Then the dragon had grabbed Sebastian and flown away.

Why? What did the dragon want? Could it really turn into a human?

The dragon stared at Sebastian for a moment longer. It felt like it was trying to say something to Sebastian, which was probably the case. So far, the dragon hadn't tried hurting Sebastian. Maybe it was trying to tell him that he wouldn't?

The dragon nodded and let go again. This time, Sebastian resisted the urge to run. Where would he go, anyway? He could head downstairs, but what were the odds that Patrick had left? The man wouldn't let him go, and Sebastian had no place to hide. He was terrified to go back home and bring Patrick with him. He didn't want to put Christian in danger.

He had to choose between taking a risk with the dragon or

doing so with Patrick, and he knew which one he'd rather do.

He raised his hands. "I'm not running away again," he promised. His voice was rough, no doubt because of the screaming.

The dragon nodded, then, to Sebastian's surprise, shifted. He watched as the dragon's body became smaller. Its form was human, but not entirely, and it was fascinating. Sebastian doubted he'd ever have the opportunity to see a dragon up close again, so he looked as much as he could without offending the dragon.

The dragon was taller than Sebastian, even in their human form. Most of their skin was the same color as Sebastian's, but there were patches of lightly colored skin that seemed to mirror the color of the dragon's hair. Sebastian couldn't see much in the darkness, but he thought it was a light blue. The dragon had wicked claws on their hands and feet, and they were entirely naked.

Sebastian found his gaze moving to the dragon's groin even though he didn't mean to. He had no idea if the dragon was male or female, and while his instinct was to say they were female because he couldn't see a cock, what did he know? He didn't see breasts, either. It could go either way, and the only way to be sure would be to ask.

He wasn't about to do that.

The dragon was beautiful. They looked otherworldly, but that didn't detract from their beauty, and Sebastian wasn't surprised to realize he was attracted to them. Who wouldn't be?

"Why did that man try to kill you?" the dragon asked.

Their voice was deep, so maybe they were a male. Should Sebastian ask for their name? Maybe that way, he'd know if he was standing with a man or a woman.

"Human," the dragon snapped. "Answer me."

"Are you going to eat me?"

The dragon stared at Sebastian as if he were an idiot. "Dragons don't eat humans."

"Really? Because I heard stories."

"Do any of your stories mention that we can turn into humans?"

"No. But then, you don't exactly turn into a human, do you? I mean, you stand on two feet, and your body is kind of human, but it's undeniable you're not." Sebastian swallowed. "If you're not going to eat me, what will you do? Will you hurt me? I saw the videos, but I thought they were fake. I couldn't have imagined that you could turn into human beings. How does it work? Does it hurt?"

The dragon pinched the bridge of their nose. Apparently, Sebastian annoyed dragons as much as he annoyed humans.

"I don't think now is the right moment to talk about dragons and how we shift," the dragon slowly said. "Tell me why the human is after you."

Right. Patrick was the reason Sebastian was on this roof with the dragon.

Sebastian looked toward the stairs. Was Patrick coming up here to get him? Or did he think that Sebastian and the dragon had flown away? Was he happy that perhaps, Sebastian was being eaten?

"Human," the dragon snapped again.

Sebastian turned his attention back to him. "I'm Sebastian."

The dragon blinked. "Sebastian. Tell me."

Sebastian sucked in a breath. "I saw him kill someone the other day. A woman. I wanted to help her, but he killed her before I could, and I hid. He found me, and I ran away, but he found me again. He doesn't want to risk me going to the cops, so he wants to kill me."

The dragon stared for a moment. Their gaze made Sebastian want to shuffle his feet, and he didn't think anyone would blame him. Of course he was nervous next to a dragon who could eat him with one bite. Plus he had no idea what was happening and what would happen next.

The dragon eventually nodded. "I'll take you somewhere else. That way, you'll be safe."

A loud *clang* somewhere in the building made Sebastian jump. He moved closer to the dragon, having decided that it was better to be eaten by a dragon shifter than to be gunned down by Patrick. At the very least, his death would be interesting.

Sebastian grabbed the dragon's arm and squeezed. The dragon looked alarmed and tried to step away, but Sebastian didn't let go.

"You'll help me?"

The dragon nodded. "That's what I just said, isn't it?"

"Thank you. I think we should go now. I can hear him."

"He's climbing the stairs," the dragon confirmed.

The dragon tried to step away again, but Sebastian needed to know something. "What's your name?"

"Is that important?"

"I don't know. I just want to know your name. You know mine, and I think I'd be more comfortable if I knew yours."

"I'm Caven."

That sounded male. "Are you a woman or a man?"

"I'm sure that isn't important."

"Maybe not, but I want to know."

"I'm a male. Can we go now?"

Sebastian nodded. He waited, but Caven just kept staring at him. Sebastian stared back until Caven pointedly looked where Sebastian was clutching his arm with both his hands. Sebastian let go as if Caven's skin had burned him. "Sorry," he muttered.

The sound of footsteps made Sebastian want to press closer to Caven, but since he knew Caven needed to shift, he didn't. He stayed where he was and watched as the dragon stepped away, then turned into the massive animal he'd been earlier.

Except it wasn't an animal. Even though that was his form now, there was humanity in him, and he showed it when he extended his arm again.

This time, Sebastian didn't hesitate. He rushed toward the dragon as the door slammed open behind him. The dragon snatched him up and pushed into the air, his massive wings extending as he did so.

Sebastian didn't scream. Even though he wanted to, he couldn't look away from the figure on the roof.

Patrick was holding an arm close to his chest, but the fact that he was hurt hadn't stopped him from trying to get to Sebastian. He carried his gun with his other hand, and he extended it toward Sebastian. He shot a few times, but Caven avoided the bullets by swinging this way and that and flying higher. When he finally moved away from the roof, Sebastian was relieved.

"I know where you live!" Patrick screamed.

Well, there went the relief Sebastian had been feeling. How did Patrick know where he lived? Would he go there right away? What about Christian?

"I need to go home," Sebastian screamed so that Caven would hear him.

Caven nodded. He was flying in a wide circle. Sebastian realized that Caven didn't know where he lived, and while it made him feel stupid, he quickly fixed that mistake. It took him a second to orient himself since he was in the air, then he pointed toward his apartment. "That way."

Caven made a grumbling sound and finally stopped flying in circles. He shot toward Sebastian's home, and Sebastian prayed he'd be fast enough to get there to save his cousin.

He didn't know what he'd do if something happened to Christian or any other member of his family. This mess was his fault, and he should be the only one in trouble for it.

Instead, he was putting his cousin in danger. He had to make sure Christian knew what was happening. He could leave the apartment for a bit, maybe go to his parents.

Sebastian didn't know what he'd do, but the first thing he needed was to make sure Christian wouldn't be caught in the crossfire when Patrick reached their apartment.

CHAPTER THREE

The human hadn't stopped talking since they'd left the roof, even though Caven couldn't hear what he was saying. Caven was relieved when they finally reached the building the human had gestured at. Clearly, this was where he lived, so Caven's mission was over.

He lowered himself, circled the roof a few times to ensure no one was there, and finally landed. He let go of Sebastian as soon as he was on the roof, but Sebastian didn't scramble away this time. Instead, he stayed there, staring at Caven as if he expected something.

Caven had never met humans until a few of them had moved in with the Ogorth clan, and even then, he'd kept his distance. He didn't know what to think of them or how to deal with them. Were all humans as puzzling as Sebastian? Or was there something special about him?

Either way, Caven's job was over, so he turned, ready to fly away.

Something grabbed his arm. He looked down to find Sebastian had wrapped himself around it and wasn't letting go. Caven frowned, then softly growled.

Nothing happened. Sebastian still clung to him, staring at him with wide eyes. Didn't he understand he needed to let go? Maybe Caven should shift and explain, but first, he raised his arm and tried to shake Sebastian off.

Sebastian clung on. "You can't go. You need to help me," he said.

Caven grumbled. Hadn't he helped Sebastian enough?

Since Sebastian didn't seem to be going anywhere, Caven shifted. In his human form, it was easier for Sebastian to cling to him, and the human took advantage of that. Caven was pretty sure he would have wrapped his legs around him, too, if he could get away with it. Instead, Sebastian held onto Caven's arm and looked up at him.

Sebastian was a beautiful man. Caven hadn't thought he could find a human beautiful, although he couldn't deny that the humans who lived with the clan were handsome. There was more than that to Sebastian, though. He looked fragile and vulnerable, and it made Caven want to protect him. He was so very different from the dragons Caven had been attracted to in the past, but Caven couldn't deny there was something there, and it was as scary as it was intriguing.

He shook his head. This wasn't what he should be thinking about.

"You need to let go," he said.

"You're abandoning me?" Sebastian's voice sounded as if he were about to cry.

Caven started panicking. What was he supposed to do if Sebastian cried?

"You have to help me, please," Sebastian begged. "I feel safe with you. I know you can protect me."

"Why should I protect you?"

Sebastian frowned. "I don't know. Why did you protect me tonight?"

"I didn't protect you. You needed help, and I didn't want you to die so close to where I live."

Sebastian's eyes widened. "So that's it? You're going to abandon my cousin and me to our fate? We didn't do anything wrong."

Why was Sebastian talking about his cousin? Caven hadn't known Sebastian had a cousin. "What are you talking about?"

"You heard Patrick. He knows where I live. I'm sure that

he's coming to my apartment even now, and I have nowhere else to go. I live with my cousin, which means he's in danger, too. If you leave me here, we're both going to die."

The old Caven wouldn't have cared. Or maybe he would have, even if he'd have tried not to let it show. Caven was tired of keeping up his mask, though. His father would have chosen words for him if he found out Caven was considering helping humans, but Caven didn't care anymore. His father wasn't here. Only Caven was, and he was the one making decisions.

"Does this Patrick know your cousin?" he asked.

"I don't think so."

"So maybe he won't kill him."

Sebastian shook his head. "He will if he finds out Christian lives with me. I told you, he wants to kill me because I saw him kill a woman. I promised I wouldn't say anything, but he didn't believe me. Either that, or he doesn't want to risk it. I just know that if you leave me here, I'll die, and so will my cousin."

"What do you expect me to do?"

"Take me with you."

Caven was already shaking his head. "I can't. I live in that abandoned building, and it would be too easy for this man to find you."

"And there isn't anywhere else you can take me?"

Caven's mind went straight to the clan. His entire life, the clan was the only place where he'd felt safe. It was the only place he'd been able to call home, and he desperately wanted to go back.

Besides, he couldn't head back to the building where he'd found Sebastian. Now that the man after Sebastian was aware that Caven lived there, he might try to hurt him. Humans might know that dragons could turn into a human form, but that didn't mean they would be any less cruel than they'd been when they'd believed dragons were merely animals.

So, Caven was homeless once again.

Sebastian grabbed Caven's hand, seemingly unafraid of his claws. "I'll give you whatever I can if you take me away. Please. I can't go to the cops because they won't care what Patrick is planning. He's always been friendly with them. I'm sure they know he's the one who killed that woman, yet they're not doing anything. They won't care if Patrick kills Christian and me. We'll just be another two deaths, and they won't even investigate. You're our only chance to make it alive, and I know it's a lot to ask, but please. Can you take us away?"

Could Caven? His first instinct was to say no, but the more he looked at Sebastian, the more he found himself wanting to say yes.

He was an idiot, and he could already imagine what his father and his other allies at the Ogorth clan would say. They'd be disgusted with him wanting to help a human, but right now, Caven didn't care. Maybe he'd never cared, even though he'd done what his father asked of him.

He didn't know anything, but of one thing, he was sure. He'd never forgive himself if something happened to Sebastian and he could have prevented it. He didn't have the clan to protect anymore, and now he found himself latching onto Sebastian, his protective instincts in overdrive.

Sebastian, who was staring at Caven with wide eyes. Sebastian, who, for some reason, seemed to trust Caven. He didn't know anything about Caven's past, and even though Caven was a dragon, he wasn't afraid of him. He seemed to believe that Caven was a good person, and for once, Caven wanted to be. He wanted to be everything Sebastian needed.

What was happening to him?

Sebastian was ready to do pretty much anything Caven wanted if it meant he'd be safe.

It would be fairly easy for Christian to move in with Sebastian's father. There was no way Christian was going home, since his parents had disowned him, but he wasn't alone, and since Patrick didn't know about him, he wasn't in as much danger as Sebastian. He would be if he stuck around, but he knew what Sebastian had seen. Sebastian was sure he could convince him to go.

But what about him? If Caven left him here, he'd die. He was sure of that. Even if he managed to run away from Patrick, eventually Patrick would find him. Besides, how was Sebastian supposed to survive on his own? If he didn't go to work, he wouldn't get paid. He didn't care about his job, but he did care about the money, and he'd need it if he was on the run.

And then there was Caven. Sebastian had always been fascinated by dragons, even before he'd found out they could turn into human beings. He had so many questions, and he wanted to ask all of them. More importantly, he just wanted to spend time with Caven. When would he have the opportunity to spend time with a dragon shifter again? This was a once-in-a-lifetime opportunity, and while he wished it hadn't happened because he'd seen a murder, sticking with Caven was the easiest way out of the situation.

That was, if Caven agreed.

"What do you expect me to do?" Caven asked.

"Take me with you."

"Where?"

Right. Caven had said that he'd been living in that abandoned building. Now that Patrick knew about it, Caven wouldn't be able to go back. "Wherever you were headed next."

"What about your cousin?"

"As long as he doesn't stay in the apartment, I think he'll be fine. He can go stay with my sister or my father."

Caven didn't ask why Christian wouldn't be staying with his own family.

Sebastian was glad for that, and it made him like Caven a little bit more. Not that he needed to like Caven more. He already liked the dragon more than should be possible. It certainly was more than was advisable.

"You're a dragon," Sebastian continued. "You already saved me once. I trust you to keep me safe more than I trust anyone else."

"You don't know me. You don't know what kind of person I am."

Something in Caven's tone told Sebastian that maybe he wouldn't like what he found out. Right now, it didn't matter. He wouldn't care even if Caven killed puppies.

Okay, maybe he *would* care if Caven killed puppies. But if Caven was cruel, he wouldn't have helped Sebastian. It would have been much easier for him to stay inside the building and wait for Patrick to be done killing him. Instead, he'd stepped in, and he'd saved Sebastian. Sebastian had to convince him to take him along wherever he was going, and he had to do it fast.

"I can pay you," he offered. "Not much, especially since I won't be able to go to work, but I have some money set aside."

Caven snorted. "I don't need your money, and I don't want it."

That was a relief. Sebastian had been ready to give Caven everything he had, but he felt better knowing he wouldn't have to. "How else am I supposed to pay you, though?" he asked. He swallowed, unsure how to feel about the thought that jumped to the front of his mind. "I guess we could, you know, do stuff. I don't have much experience, but you could guide me through it."

Caven stared. "What are you talking about?"

"You know, sex. I've never had sex with a dragon, but I'm sure it can work."

"You're offering to have sex with me so I'll help you?"

"I don't know how else to convince you."

"Not by offering me sex. I have dragons throwing themselves at me left and right."

Sebastian almost laughed at how indignant Caven sounded. "Well, that's great. What do you want from me, then?"

"Nothing."

That didn't sound good, but Sebastian needed help. "What about your people?"

Caven's eyes narrowed. "What about them?"

"Well, if you don't want to help me, maybe they can." Sebastian didn't know if dragons lived in families like humans, and he didn't care right now. He just needed someone, preferably a dragon, to help him.

"You don't believe I can help you?"

"It's more that you don't look like you *want* to help me."

"I'll help you because you need someone to help you. I don't expect payment, and I don't need you to find another dragon."

It sounded too good to be true, but Sebastian couldn't afford to overthink this right now.

The sound of a screeching car made him jump. He rushed to the edge of the roof only to see Patrick scrambling out of a badly parked car.

Sebastian was out of time.

He turned to face Caven. "It's Patrick."

He was thankful when Caven took control.

"Call your cousin. Tell him he needs to pack a bag and get out of your apartment. He has to act as if he doesn't live with you and like he's not afraid or expecting something to go wrong. Tell him you'll give him more details as soon as it's safe."

Sebastian nodded and took his phone out of his pocket. He fumbled with it and almost dropped it, but Caven snatched it out of his hands, waited for a second to be sure Sebastian had steadied himself, and gave it back. Sebastian didn't have to look for his cousin's number because he knew it by heart, and he quickly dialed it. As he listened to the ringing, he prayed Christian would answer quickly.

"Are you still at the grocery store?" Christian asked when he did.

"I need you to listen to me," Sebastian said. "Patrick O'Neill found me at the grocery store. He came after me, and while I managed to escape, he knows where I live. I need you to pack a bag and go to my father's. You have to be quick because Patrick is already here."

"What are you talking about?"

"Please," Sebastian begged. "I'll call you again as soon as I'm safe. I promise. I don't want you to get hurt because of me."

"You're not kidding."

"I'm not. Please, go to my father. Take the stairs. Patrick is wounded, so hopefully, he'll need the elevator. You have to be out of the building in less than five minutes."

"I want an explanation once this is over," Christian warned.

"I promise I'll give you one."

"Are you safe?"

Sebastian peered at Caven, who was still staring down at the street. "As safe as I can be. Patrick didn't hurt me."

"Call me. I'll be waiting for your phone call, and I'm sure your father will be, too, once I tell him what's been happening."

Sebastian groaned, but he knew better than to think he

could keep his father out of this. "I'll tell you everything you need to know as soon as everyone is safe."

Christian didn't waste any more time. He hung up, and Sebastian turned to Caven. "He'll be out of here soon."

Caven nodded. "He needs to be fast because that man is in the building."

Sebastian went to stand next to Caven and looked down. From their position, he could see the street but not the entrance of the building. Patrick was nowhere to be seen, and Sebastian held his breath as he waited for either him or Christian to appear.

His knees buckled in relief when his cousin appeared a few minutes later. He was carrying two bags, and after looking left and right, he quickly walked down the street to his car. Sebastian held his breath, but nothing else happened. Christian got into his car, turned it on, and drove off.

He was safe.

"I can hear the elevator," Caven said. "I think Patrick suspects you're on the roof."

That would make sense, since Sebastian had flown off with a dragon. "We need to go, then."

Caven nodded, but he didn't move. He seemed to be torn or something, and Sebastian prayed that something wasn't whether or not he should help him.

Caven had already decided he'd take Sebastian to the clan. Even if the clan didn't welcome him back, they wouldn't cast out a human in danger.

Or at least, that was what Caven was trying to convince himself of.

Before they left, he needed Sebastian to know a few things. He faced the human while also keeping an ear open for the elevator. It was coming closer, which meant that the man who'd tried killing Sebastian was almost there. It would be easy for Caven to kill the human, and he was tempted to do so, but for some reason, he didn't want Sebastian to be afraid of him or to see him as a monster.

"I'll be taking you to my clan," he said.

Sebastian's eyes went round. "You have a clan?"

"I do." Not anymore, but Sebastian didn't need to know that. "But it's not close. We'll have to travel for several days, which means we'll have to sleep in the forest. It won't be comfortable."

"I don't need it to be comfortable. I just need to get out of here."

That was all Caven needed to hear. He shifted back to his dragon form with a nod and held out his hand. Sebastian didn't hesitate to step closer, which surprised Caven. Shouldn't Sebastian be at least a bit afraid of him? He could kill the human with one movement, yet Sebastian didn't seem to realize that, or maybe he did but didn't care.

Spending time in the human world hadn't made humans easier to understand.

Instead of holding Sebastian in his hand like he'd done the previous two times they'd flown together, Caven twisted and dropped Sebastian onto his back. Sebastian almost fell off, and Caven had to press his head against the human's ass to push him back into place. By the time Sebastian settled down, the elevator had reached the upper floor and stopped. Caven heard the door open, and he readied himself to shoot up into the air.

Sebastian clung to Caven's back as Caven moved. It wasn't very secure, but it was the best Caven could offer for now. They'd find a way to tie Sebastian to Caven the next time they stopped. It wouldn't be long, anyway. It was late at night, and Caven didn't trust humans enough to want to fly during the day. That meant that they'd have to land before too long and spend the day resting and sleeping.

But they shouldn't start this trip without food or other things they might need. If he'd been alone, Caven would have been able to take care of himself, but he wasn't. He had no idea what the human needed, but they were more fragile than dragons. He didn't want to break Sebastian, which meant he'd have to stop somewhere so that Sebastian could buy some of the things he would need.

But for now, Caven took to the air, leaving the building behind. He heard the sound of a door slamming as he flew away, but he didn't turn to check who it was. The wind caught his wings, carrying him up, and he closed his eyes for a moment.

He'd always loved flying. It allowed him to be away from his family and his father. In the air, he didn't have to be anyone but himself. It was the only place where he was truly free, or at least, it had been until he'd left the clan.

And now, he was going back.

He was doing it because Sebastian needed help. It wouldn't do to leave him on his own, and Caven couldn't think of anyone else who could help him. The clan was Sebastian's best option, and Caven hoped he wouldn't regret it. Maybe his cousin would allow him to leave again once he got there. He didn't expect the clan to welcome him back, but at the very least, they'd welcome Sebastian. Even after Caven left or was placed behind bars again, they'd protect him.

Because those were Caven's only two options. He'd left, thinking it was the best thing for him, but being away from the clan had shown him just how lonely he was without it. He'd always done his best to protect the clan from his father's plans, and while he hadn't been able to do anything from his cell, at least there he'd been close enough to know what was happening. In the human world, he had no idea what was going on with the clan since he'd left.

But not for long. He was going home, and at this point, he didn't even care that his home would be a cell.

CHAPTER FOUR

Sebastian wished Caven could answer his questions while he was in his dragon form, but clearly, he couldn't. He would already have talked to Sebastian if he could talk in his dragon form, right?

Sebastian had so many questions. He wanted to know how the shift worked and if it hurt. He wanted to know which form Caven preferred. Sebastian loved the dragon, but he couldn't deny that he felt closer to Caven when Caven was in his human form. Could dragons communicate when they were dragons? Or could they only do that when they were in their human form?

Thinking about the many questions he had helped Sebastian not look down. He probably should have mentioned to Caven that he was terrified of heights. If he looked down, he might faint, which was the worst thing that could happen while straddling a dragon's back.

So instead of opening his eyes, he talked.

Caven didn't say anything about it, so Sebastian hoped it meant he didn't mind. After a while, Sebastian's voice turned rough, so he had to stop talking anyway. They were still flying, and he was still clutching whatever part of Caven he could hold on to. He suspected Caven would be able to grab him if he fell, but he wasn't about to risk finding out the hard way.

He finally opened his eyes when he felt the air around him warm. He realized it was because the sun was coming up, which probably meant they'd have to land soon. He carefully avoided looking at the ground and instead stared at the sunrise. He'd never seen it from this position, and he didn't think he ever would again.

It was beautiful.

The sky around them was losing its darkness, the blacks and blues turning to deep purples. It would be a beautiful day, although Sebastian didn't know if that would be true for him. Whatever happened, he was safer than he would have been if he'd stayed back home. If he had, he'd probably already be dead, so every day more he had was a treasure.

A treasure he owed to Caven.

Sebastian gently patted the skin of Caven's neck. He'd expected it to be rough, but it was smooth and warm. He didn't want to bother Caven, so he didn't touch him again, but it felt good to reassure himself that he was riding a dragon in the middle of the sky. He wasn't dreaming, and he wasn't dead.

Eventually, Caven tilted forward. Sebastian slammed his eyes shut again and clung harder to the spikes that ran down Caven's back. They weren't the most comfortable, but he managed to stay in place as they landed. Even once they had, he stayed where he was, his eyes still shut. He took a deep breath, then another, and reminded himself that everything was all right. He was on the ground again, and he was safe.

A grunt made him open his eyes. Caven had twisted his neck around and was staring at Sebastian. He looked from Sebastian to the ground, and Sebastian's cheeks flushed as he finally let go.

"Sorry," he muttered.

He slid off Caven's back and instantly fell to the ground. His knees were weak, and he felt like he'd run a marathon. He wasn't sure his legs could hold him up, so instead, he crossed his legs and looked at Caven, who was shifting into his human form.

Watching the shift was incredible and not something

Sebastian had ever expected to see. It was smooth and seemed easy, and there was no sign of pain in Caven as he did so.

Once Caven was in his human form, he raised his arms and stretched, and Sebastian had to look away. He didn't want to seem like a creep, even though he felt like one. He was glad to be able to see Caven's color now, though. He'd seen Caven's dragon form was turquoise when they were flying, and the color carried over to Caven's human form. Caven's short hair was turquoise, as were his eyes and the patches of scaly skin that peppered his body.

But since Sebastian didn't want to be caught staring, he glanced at the area where they'd landed. They were in the middle of a forest. Everywhere Sebastian looked, the only things he could see were trees, trees, and more trees. Caven had mentioned his clan, and Sebastian supposed it made sense for dragons to live away from humans. They could fly, so they wouldn't have a problem getting home, but it would take humans days to get there, which was more than enough time for dragons to notice them.

Sebastian had never spent much time in nature, but there was a first time for everything. He kind of wished his first time in a forest hadn't been because he was running for his life, but he'd make do.

"We need to stop for the day," Caven said. "That way, people won't notice us. I wanted to stop somewhere to get you some food, but I felt it would be better to put more space between you and the man who tried to kill you instead. I'll hunt something later tonight if that's okay with you."

"I'm fine." Sebastian was hungry, but he could deal with it for a bit longer. The sensation reminded him that he was alive.

Caven nodded. "Good. We should try to get some sleep, then."

Sebastian looked around. The forest ground wasn't going to be comfortable, but he didn't have a choice, so he'd make do.

His eyes widened when Caven shifted again. He watched as the dragon circled the small area between the trees where they'd landed, seemed to find the perfect spot, and curled into a tight ball. It was kind of like watching a dog picking the best spot to sleep, and it was endearing.

But that left Sebastian not knowing where to sleep.

He got to his knees and poked around for a bit, trying to find the softest place, but everything was hard. He could certainly sleep there, but it wouldn't be easy.

He eyed Caven. The dragon was already asleep, or at least, he looked like he was. Would he notice if Sebastian curled up next to him? At the very least, being close to him would keep Sebastian warm.

But before going to bed, Sebastian needed to do something. He took out his phone, relieved to see he had one little bar on the signal symbol. He couldn't call his father, but he could text him, and he did so. He wanted his dad and Christian to know he was okay and for them not to be alarmed when he didn't come home. Eventually, he would, but for now he was on an adventure he hoped would never end. He didn't even care about Patrick anymore. As long as Patrick O'Neill left his family alone, Sebastian would be fine never going back.

Since he wasn't sure how long it would take them to reach Caven's clan, Sebastian turned off his phone. After poking around on the ground for a bit longer, he decided he'd never get any sleep if he had to stretch out on the ground by himself. So he shuffled on his knees until he reached Caven. He gently poked at the dragon, and when Caven didn't react, he stretched out next to him. He pressed as close to Caven as he dared, holding his breath when Caven moved. Caven's warmth radiated against his body, and he found himself smiling.

He had no idea what the future held for him, and he

wished he hadn't seen that poor woman getting killed, but it had led to him meeting Caven. Caven was a revelation, something Sebastian had never expected would happen to him, and he couldn't find it in himself to be angry at the situation when it had given him Caven.

Caven stayed as still as possible. He wasn't even sure he was breathing.

What was Sebastian doing?

Caven had curled up to sleep, but he'd been keeping an ear open to make sure Sebastian didn't go wander off in the forest. He'd heard him move around for a bit, and unless he was mistaken, Sebastian had texted someone. Caven had thought he'd finally go to sleep after that, but instead, Sebastian had settled down against him.

Why?

There were two options—either Caven stayed where he was and acted as if he was asleep, or he pushed Sebastian away and told him to keep his distance. Caven knew which one would be smarter, but he also knew which one he wanted, no matter how much it didn't make sense.

He stayed quiet and still.

He still couldn't understand why Sebastian wasn't afraid of him. Even though Caven was in his dragon form, the human didn't hesitate to burrow against his stomach. He pressed his face against the skin there, which tickled, but Caven stayed still anyway. He was surprised to realize he *wanted* Sebastian to feel comfortable with him. He wanted Sebastian not to be afraid of him, even though he didn't understand why.

Well, maybe he did understand.

With Sebastian, Caven had a fresh start. Sebastian didn't know who Caven was and what he'd done. He didn't think

Caven was a traitor. Everyone else in Caven's life had believed that, and maybe they hadn't been wrong. Maybe, no matter how hard Caven had been trying to help the clan, they could only see the way he'd gone about it.

But that didn't matter now. The only thing that mattered was that Sebastian was falling asleep against Caven, looking entirely relaxed and at peace. Even after what happened to him, after being pushed to run away from his home and his family, he was still calm and bubbly. Caven wouldn't have believed anyone who told him that humans were as resilient as they clearly were, but he had proof snuggled against him.

And Sebastian wasn't the only one. Caven had seen how strong the two humans who'd moved in with the clan were. It would have been easier for them to stay away, but instead, they'd become full members of the Ogorth clan, and the clan had come to rely on them. One of them was teaching the queen's son, while the other was in charge of everything computer related and security. Sheldon even had a child with Morven, which most people hadn't believed was possible.

Caven softly snorted. He'd never forget his father's face the day he'd found out that Morven and Sheldon's daughter had hatched and that she was perfect. It was even more than that — not only did she look perfect, but she could shift back and forth between her dragon and her human form, even though she'd just been born. Dragons couldn't do that. Apparently, human-dragon hybrids could, and Caven's father had been *pissed*. He'd ranted about how humans didn't belong with the clan and shouldn't sully dragons' legacies for hours, and Caven had been forced to listen to him.

He was happy for Morven and Sheldon. He was happy their daughter was all right, but he'd kept his distance in spite of how much he wanted to tell them that. Showing any kind of attention to them that wasn't disgust or animosity would have drawn the interest of Caven's father, which was the last thing anyone needed.

It was better for Sheldon and Morven to stay away from Caven's father, just like it was better for Caven to do so.

Sebastian gave a little snore and pushed even closer. He rubbed his nose against Caven's stomach, and Caven looked down at him, wondering if he was doing it on purpose.

Caven couldn't forget that Sebastian had offered him sex to entice him to help him. He couldn't deny that for a split second, he'd been tempted to accept. Once he was back with the clan, there wouldn't be any opportunity for him to have sex.

But he didn't want Sebastian to feel like he had to do it. If Sebastian wanted to have sex with him, Caven would be more than happy to do so. If Sebastian just wanted to thank him, though, Caven could do without it.

Sebastian was asleep. His eyes were closed, and he was breathing regularly.

Caven relaxed. His thoughts went back to what would happen once he was back at the palace. He'd be taken back to his cell, but what about Sebastian? The clan wouldn't hurt him, but Caven wouldn't be able to see him again. Even though they'd just met, he could already tell he'd miss Sebastian's personality and happiness. He wanted more of it, and he wanted more of feeling normal. He wanted a second chance, and even though it surprised him, he wanted it with Sebastian.

His father would be *so* pissed if he ever found out about this.

The thought made Caven smile, and he continued smiling as he fell asleep. It didn't matter if he was put back in his cell right away. The entire clan would know he'd arrived with a human, which meant his father would find out. He'd know Caven had spent time with a human and that they were close, and he might even suspect there was more between Caven and Sebastian than there was.

Caven wished he could be there to see his father's head explode.

CHAPTER FIVE

They were almost there.

When Caven opened his eyes three days after he and Sebastian had fled the city, it was with those words on his mind. They were almost there, which meant that Caven's time with Sebastian was almost over.

He looked down. Sebastian was still curled up against him, sleeping as if he didn't have a worry in the world. Maybe he didn't, not beyond the guy trying to kill him. Spending time with him had been fun, and it had shown Caven that maybe his life could be different. Sebastian didn't hesitate to talk about his family, the people he loved, and his life back in the city. Caven had never known anyone like him, and it was his fault.

He could have become friends with Blake and Sheldon. He could have become friends with Cain. Instead, he'd acted like an asshole, and he was still paying the price. He'd thought that leaving would mean he would be free, but instead he kept thinking about the clan and how it was his home, even though everyone in the clan hated him.

And now they were almost home, and Caven's time with Sebastian was about to end.

He carefully extracted himself from Sebastian's grasp. It wasn't easy, but the human was a heavy sleeper, and Caven had warned him not to freak out if he didn't find him when he woke up in the evening. Caven had to take care of Sebastian, which meant hunting. He'd rather do that when there was still a little light around, so he left Sebastian behind and

44

headed into the forest.

He recognized it now. He knew that the clan would realize someone was approaching in just a few hours. They'd probably be able to find Caven on the cameras, which meant they'd know he was coming. Hopefully, it also meant they'd know he was coming with someone and that they would refrain from attacking him in the air. Caven wasn't a fighter, and while he knew how to defend himself, he couldn't win a fight in the air.

He swallowed. It wouldn't come to that. If it did, he'd do his best to protect Sebastian and to make sure he made it to the clan. That was Caven's only goal now, and he had every intention of fulfilling it.

He managed to catch a few rabbits. It wouldn't be enough for his dragon, but he'd get food soon anyway. In the meantime, Sebastian would be fed, which was Caven's main goal. He made his way toward the trees under which they'd slept, but he couldn't see Sebastian when he got there.

He dropped the rabbits on the ground and shifted, his heart racing. "Sebastian?" he called out.

Had Caven gotten it wrong? Was he in the wrong area of the forest? But no. He could smell Sebastian's presence, which meant he'd been here until recently. Had someone taken him?

"Sebastian?" Caven called again, louder this time.

Something moved behind one of the trees, and Sebastian's face appeared. He was so pale that Caven knew something had happened, and he rushed toward him. When he grabbed him, Sebastian threw himself into his arms without hesitation. He wrapped his arms around Caven's neck and held on, and Caven could only hold him back.

"What happened?" Caven asked. He buried his face against Sebastian's hair and took a deep breath. He hadn't realized how terrified he was until he had Sebastian back in his arms, but now, he did.

What was *happening* to him?

"I heard noises," Sebastian said.

"We're in a forest. You're bound to hear noises." Caven gently tried to push Sebastian away, but Sebastian wouldn't move. If anything, he clung harder to Caven, almost as if he wanted to become one with him.

"I thought you'd decided I wasn't worth the bother and that you'd left," Sebastian said.

"Why would I leave you? I told you I'd take you to my clan, and I'll do just that."

"But I still don't understand why. I'm just a human. What can I give your clan that would persuade them to allow me to stay with you? I just know that once we get there, you'll realize how pathetic I am, and you'll throw me back into the forest."

Caven awkwardly patted Sebastian's back. He wasn't sure what else to do to comfort him. "We don't throw useless people in the forest. If we did, half the clan would be gone."

Sebastian chuckled, but it still didn't sound as happy as it should. What else could Caven say?

It didn't help that he was distracted by Sebastian's closeness. His body was reacting to the human, and Caven didn't want to freak him out. He doubted Sebastian had any idea how sex worked with dragons, even dragons in their human form.

When humans had moved in with the clan, Caven had done some research. He'd been curious, especially after Morven had gotten pregnant. He knew the differences between the human and dragon bodies and that there would be no way for him to hide how he felt about Sebastian if Sebastian stayed in his arms.

He tried to push Sebastian away again, but Sebastian continued to be clingy.

"We have a few humans with us," Caven said, desperate.

Sebastian looked up at him, blinking. "You do?"

"Yes. Two brothers, and both of them are dating clan members."

Sebastian's eyes widened. "They have sex with dragons?"

Caven had no idea if Sebastian was doing it on purpose, but he pushed even closer. Their bodies were plastered together, which meant there was no way that Sebastian didn't feel it when Caven's cock slid out of its pouch.

Caven was desperate to distract Sebastian, so he blathered on. "One of them even has a child with one of our dragons," he said, trying to tilt his hips away from Sebastian. "No one knew if it would work in the beginning. There has been no other dragon-human hybrid as far as we can remember."

Sebastian snorted. "That's ridiculous."

"Why is it ridiculous?"

"Because if any human has ever known about dragons and their human form, they'd have tried to fuck you. It's what we do."

Caven laughed. "So humans are sexually adventurous?"

Sebastian looked up at Caven from under his lashes. He bit his lower lip, and once again, Caven wondered if he was doing it on purpose. Did he know how appealing he was? Was he trying to seduce Caven, or was he behaving like this because it was how he always behaved?

"We like to stick our dicks in whatever spot where it could fit."

Then Sebastian did something that Caven knew was deliberate. Still looking at Caven, he pressed his hips forward again.

And Caven realized he wasn't the only one aroused.

Sebastian's cock was hard in his jeans. There was no mistaking that, no matter how many times Caven told himself it wasn't possible. Sebastian wanted him, and he was making it very obvious. He was also giving Caven a way out. If Caven didn't want this, he could just step away. Sebastian wouldn't force him to do anything.

But Caven was so tired of resisting.

Back at home, he couldn't be with the people he wanted. Instead, he had to be with whoever was more fitting for what his father had planned for him, which was taking his cousin's place on the throne. That didn't mean Caven never had sex with anyone, but he had to do it in secret, and he never allowed himself to completely lose himself in it.

But Sebastian wouldn't hurt him. He wouldn't hold anything against Caven, and he wouldn't attempt to blackmail him. It wasn't the kind of person he was, and right now, he felt like the perfect person to give in with.

Sebastian seemed to have had enough of Caven's hesitation. He pressed forward and tilted his head, making his intention clear. Caven held his breath as their lips brushed together.

It was like something sparked in him. As soon as Sebastian kissed him, he found himself wanting more, and his body reacted as if it had a mind of its own. His hands slid down Sebastian's back to grab his ass, and he hauled Sebastian up.

Sebastian laughed and wrapped himself around Caven, then kissed him a second time.

Once again, Caven had no idea what was happening, but for the first time, he didn't care. He'd take whatever Sebastian gave him, and he'd do it with pleasure.

The first day Sebastian had awakened snuggled against Caven, he'd expected the dragon to say something about it. Caven was prickly, and Sebastian had been sure he'd tell him to fuck off and keep his distance. Instead, Caven had acted as if nothing had happened and as if they hadn't woken up snuggled in each other's arms.

Well, Sebastian had been in Caven's arms. It would have been a bit hard for Sebastian to wrap his arms around Caven's dragon form.

But Caven had behaved as if nothing had been wrong, so Sebastian had, too. Caven had hunted. Then, as soon as they'd eaten, they'd gotten back on the road. They'd followed the same schedule the following two days, and this morning, after they'd landed, Caven had said they were nearly at the clan.

Sebastian was nervous. He felt fine when it was only Caven, but he didn't know what to expect from an entire dragon clan. Would they even want him there? Caven had told him it wouldn't be a problem, but Sebastian wasn't so sure. He supposed it would be more interesting to die because a dragon had eaten him than from being shot by an asshole, but still. If he could avoid it, he'd rather stay alive.

Staying alive could lead to more exciting ways of eating Sebastian.

When Sebastian had woken up tonight, he'd been alone. That was the first time it happened, and he'd freaked out. He'd been convinced Caven had finally come to his senses and abandoned him. Then he'd heard a noise, and his brain had told him he was about to be eaten — and not in a fun way. So he'd hidden.

But once again, Caven had saved him, and Sebastian had stopped resisting the attraction that had been growing between them. It seemed that Caven had, too, because he was clutching at Sebastian's body as if he were desperate to get him naked.

They stumbled, making Sebastian squeak, but he shouldn't have worried. Caven had been saving him since the first time they'd met, and tonight wasn't any different. He got his footing, and he started moving.

Sebastian's back hit a tree, making him wince, but he couldn't have cared less about the slight pain. It disappeared next to what Caven was doing to him.

Sebastian had thought he'd be the one the most into this. He'd been attracted to Caven since the night they'd met, and that attraction had grown over the past few days. Caven had kept him at a distance, which was why Sebastian hadn't believed he wanted him as much as Sebastian did.

Clearly, he'd been wrong.

With Sebastian's back pressed against the tree, Caven could focus on things besides trying to keep upright. Sebastian could, too, and he couldn't ignore what was between them.

Caven's cock.

Over the days, Sebastian had allowed himself to sneak peeks at Caven. He'd been curious about Caven's human body, and now he knew how it worked. He'd been confused in the beginning, but it was clear that Caven had a cock. It had been hidden, but it wasn't anymore.

Far from it.

It pressed against Sebastian's, making him feel like he'd go nuts if he didn't get out of his jeans. He wasn't afraid to let go of Caven's neck, because he knew Caven would hold him up.

He did. Caven pushed harder against Sebastian, making Sebastian lose track for a few seconds. He didn't know what to do. He wanted Caven's cock inside of him, but they didn't have lube, so that wouldn't be possible. He was up to trying pretty much anything, but being fucked without lube wasn't on top of his list.

He reached between him and Caven and opened his jeans. The problem was that now that they were open, he couldn't get them off. The only thing he managed to do was hook them under his balls, along with his underwear. It wasn't exactly comfortable, but it would do. It wasn't like Caven needed to be anywhere near his ass.

As he raised his hands again, the back of his knuckles

brushed against the opening at Caven's groin. Caven's cock jutted from it, but that wasn't what surprised Sebastian.

It was the slickness.

Knowing Caven wouldn't hesitate to tell him if he was doing something he disliked, Sebastian tentatively wrapped his fingers around Caven's cock. It was big and smooth, smoother than a human's. It was also so slick that if Sebastian hadn't known better, he would have thought Caven had lube stashed somewhere.

He explored Caven's cock as Caven mauled his neck, jaw, and lips. He was kissing and nibbling on every inch of skin he could get to, which wasn't a lot, considering Sebastian was still fully dressed. Sebastian didn't care, though. He felt that he'd have already come if he'd been naked.

That was how much he wanted Caven.

Sebastian slid his fingers down the length of Caven's cock. He explored the area where it was rooted in the slit, and then he slipped a finger inside.

Caven groaned and shuddered.

Clearly that was welcome, and Sebastian felt smug that he was able to give Caven what he needed. The smugness quickly vanished, replaced by awe, surprise, and lust.

Sebastian hadn't been joking when he'd said that humans wanted to stick their cocks wherever they could fit. As he felt inside Caven, making him shiver and groan, he wondered if his cock would fit there. He was willing to try, but he didn't want to make Caven run.

But his cock felt like it was about to explode if he didn't do something soon, and he wanted Caven to feel pleasure as much as he did.

Suddenly, Caven pushed away from the tree. Sebastian just had the time to wrap his arms around Caven's neck, but they didn't go far. Caven dropped to his knees, turning so Sebastian wouldn't hit the tree.

Then, to Sebastian's surprise, Caven dragged him along as he stretched out on his back.

Sebastian ended up between Caven's legs, his cock pressed next to Caven's. His first instinct was to push and enter Caven, but he took a moment to look at the dragon under him.

He was beautiful.

His cheeks were a shade darker than their usual turquoise, and his eyes were wide. His lips had parted, and he stared back.

Sebastian continued his visual exploration.

Caven's long limbs were on the ground, his legs splayed, welcoming Sebastian. His cock glistened in the dimming light of the day, and his pouch was slightly open. There was a darker line on his stomach, from his pouch to his belly button.

Sebastian wanted to explore Caven's entire body with his fingers and tongue. He wanted to give Caven so much more than a fuck in the woods, and he wasn't about to say no to whatever was about to happen, but it wouldn't be the only time it happened between them. Sebastian wouldn't that when Caven deserved to be cherished and taken care of. It was odd to think that way, because Caven had been taking care of Sebastian since they left the city, but it was how Sebastian felt.

He tried to speak, had to pause to clear his throat, then finally managed to get the words out. "I'm not sure what you expect from me."

Caven reached for Sebastian with both hands. Sebastian went easily, quickly pushing his jeans down his thighs as he slotted between Caven's legs.

"There's enough space in the pouch for you to take me," Caven said. His voice was rough.

Sebastian smiled at the realization that Caven was as much into this as he was. He kissed Caven, then settled against him. "Only if you take me the next time we do this."

An emotion Sebastian couldn't read flashed on Caven's face. It was gone as quickly as it had appeared, though, and Caven nodded. "Next time we do this, I'll take you," he promised.

That was good enough for Sebastian. He wiggled his hips until the head of his cock brushed against Caven's pouch. He sucked in a breath, then gently pushed in.

He hadn't thought of asking Caven if he needed to stretch him, but he realized he didn't as he entered Caven's body. Caven was slick and welcoming, and there were no signs of resistance. Sebastian pushed in until his hips were flush against Caven's. Caven's cock pulsed between them, and every time Sebastian moved into Caven, he could feel it rubbing against his stomach. Caven's head was thrown back, and his hands were probably leaving imprints on Sebastian's shoulders.

Sebastian didn't care.

Caven could leave as many signs on his body as he wanted. Sebastian would wear them proudly, just like he wouldn't hesitate to claim Caven as his own.

Caven looked at him, and Sebastian couldn't resist. He kissed him as he fucked into him, grinning at the sounds Caven was making. He couldn't believe he was the one giving Caven so much pleasure, and he never wanted this to end. He didn't know if it would or if he and Caven would have the opportunity to be together once they were with Caven's clan, but he had every intention of making sure they did.

Caven cried out into Sebastian's mouth. Sebastian moved faster, his orgasm growing. His entire body felt like it was tingling, but he wanted Caven to come first.

He *needed* Caven to come first. He needed to show Caven he could take care of him. So Sebastian fucked him harder and faster until finally Caven came between them. It slicked both their bodies, and Sebastian wished he'd taken off his t-shirt.

Then he didn't care about anything but what his cock was doing, and he came, filling a place deep inside Caven's body.

Sebastian's movements slowed down, then stopped. Both he and Caven were still panting and breathing heavily, and for a moment, everything was perfect. Sebastian kissed the side of Caven's neck, and Caven made a rumbling sound that might have been a purr.

Did dragons purr?

Sebastian pushed himself up and rolled next to Caven into a sitting position. Caven got up, too, and while it seemed he couldn't look Sebastian in the eyes, Sebastian didn't care. He grabbed one of Caven's hands and kissed its back, smiling like an idiot.

"You promised me a next time," he said.

Caven hesitated, then nodded. "And if I can, I'll keep that promise."

That was all Sebastian wanted. He and Caven hadn't talked about being together, but after what they'd done, he decided that he'd behave as if they were. If Caven had a problem with that, he'd tell him. He was never shy with his opinions.

Sebastian's life might be in danger, but he'd gotten a dragon boyfriend out of it.

Maybe being hunted by a killer wasn't so bad, after all.

CHAPTER SIX

Even as he flew, Caven couldn't stop thinking about what he and Sebastian had done in the forest. He didn't think he'd ever be able to stop thinking about it.

He still wasn't sure what had gotten into him. A few weeks ago, he would have been horrified at the thought of having sex with a human. Yet now, he couldn't wait to do it again.

Or maybe he wouldn't have been horrified. His father certainly would be, but Caven had never hated humans, even though he'd said and done whatever his father wanted him to say and do. He was afraid they'd hurt the clan, and he was careful, but he was also curious.

He wasn't an idiot. He knew that just like there were good and bad dragons—his father came to mind as one of the bad ones—there were good and bad humans. Not all humans wanted to hunt and kill dragons, and Sebastian didn't. Neither did Blake and Sheldon, for that matter.

But Caven had never been allowed to show any interest in them or to get to know them. His father would have made sure he regretted it, and it had been safer for everyone to act as if Caven hated them.

He regretted that. He regretted many things he'd done because his father had pushed him, and now he was going to have to face all of it all over again.

He could see the palace in the distance. He wasn't sure Sebastian had noticed it yet, but it meant their time together was coming to an end. Caven should have told Sebastian that he'd be arrested as soon as he reached the palace, but he hadn't wanted to ruin what little time they still had not attempt to step between Caven and the guards. Caven didn't want him to be hurt, especially not because of him.

Over the sound of the wind, he heard Sebastian suck in a breath. He'd seen the palace, finally.

"Is that where your clan lives?" Sebastian yelled.

Caven nodded, since he couldn't say anything. It was probably better that way, anyway. Once they reached the palace, Sebastian could become friends with Sheldon and Blake, and they'd no doubt tell him what Caven had done. Then Sebastian wouldn't want anything to do with him again, and he'd be able to continue on with his life. What had happened between them had been good, and Caven wanted it to happen again, but it wasn't the best thing for Sebastian.

"It looks incredible," Sebastian said.

It did. It was one of the reasons it had been so crucial to Caven to keep the clan safe. The palace was his home, the place where he was born, and probably the place where he'd die. He'd thought it would be the place where he'd have a family, too, but that wasn't in the cards anymore.

For years, he'd fooled himself into thinking that he was doing what his father asked of him because it was the only way for the clan to survive. He needed to be on the throne, and once he was, his father would have helped him save the clan.

But it all been a lie. The only reason his father wanted to put him on the throne was that he wanted to manipulate him. He wanted power, but he didn't wish to be open about it. It had been easy to use Caven, and by the time Caven had realized how wrong his father was and that the clan was in safe hands with Ita, it had been too late.

He'd done his best not to hurt any of the people he'd been ordered to deal with. He'd made sure to send only the stupidest people after Sheldon and Blake, and when he'd taken Cain, he'd had a backup plan. He wouldn't have let Cain's old clan take him, but he hadn't tried to explain any of this to anyone. They wouldn't have believed him.

Hell, he wouldn't have believed himself if he'd been in their position.

He wouldn't try to explain this time around, either. He didn't deserve to have Cain and the others forgive him, and he did deserve to be locked up. His stunt in the human world had been stupid, but he'd wanted to be free. Now he realized that wasn't true. He didn't want to be free, at least not from the clan. He wanted to be away from his father and to be home, and he'd get both those things in his cell.

His mouth went dry as he reached the palace. He headed up the mountain toward the landing pad. He had no doubt people would already be there waiting for him, so he wasn't surprised when, once he reached the highest spot of the mountain and started going down inside, he saw the pad was full of people.

He still landed. It would have been easy for him to fly away, but instead, he aimed for the middle of the pad, and when his feet hit the ground, he and Sebastian were surrounded. The guards didn't come closer. They kept their distance, and Caven gently helped Sebastian climb off his back. He was glad the guards weren't attacking him on sight. He'd have fought to protect Sebastian, but he didn't want to have to.

Sebastian slid off Caven's back. Caven made sure he was steady on his feet, and when he pressed his muzzle against Sebastian's stomach, Sebastian chuckled and rubbed his nose.

"You're home," he said.

Caven's heart broke a little. Yes, he was home.

Sebastian hadn't known what to expect when Caven talked about his clan, but it wasn't for them to live in a freaking palace.

The place where they'd landed wasn't as beautiful as the palace he'd seen as they approached it, but he supposed that made sense. This space was clearly made for dragons to land and take off, and it needed to be practical more than beautiful.

He looked around. There was stone everywhere he could see, from the ground to the walls carved into the mountain. But that wasn't what caught his attention.

Why were all these dragons circling them?

He leaned against Caven. "Is something wrong?"

Caven shifted and wrapped an arm around Sebastian's waist. "Everything will be fine," he promised.

Sebastian didn't believe him. The guards parted, and a tall green dragon stepped through. A black one followed, and Sebastian couldn't look away.

They were bigger than Caven. They were in their human form, and just like Caven, their color carried over their entire body. The black one looked pissed, and before he could think better about it, Sebastian moved and placed himself between the black dragon and Caven.

The black dragon's eyebrows shot up on his forehead. He looked at the green dragon, who turned back to look at Sebastian.

"Don't," Caven said.

He tried pulling Sebastian back, but Sebastian wasn't moving. If these dragons were going to hurt Caven, they'd have to go through him first.

Not that it would be hard. They could shift and eat Sebastian in one bite.

"Caven," the green dragon said. "We didn't expect you to come back."

"I didn't expect to come back, either," Caven said.

The green dragon nodded. "You'll be taken back to your cell."

He moved his hands, and two of the dragons circling them stepped forward. Sebastian panicked. He didn't know what to do, but he had to do *something*. Standing in front of Caven wasn't helping, so instead, he did one of the stupidest things he'd ever done.

He turned around and wrapped himself around Caven.

Caven made a surprised sound, but when Sebastian wrapped both of his arms and one leg around him, he hugged him back. It was awkward, but if these dragons were going to take Caven, they'd have to drag Sebastian away.

"Sebastian, you have to let go," Caven said.

Sebastian shook his head. The movement made his cheek rub against Caven's chest, which Sebastian would have been delighted by in any other circumstance.

"Please," Caven said. "I don't want you to be hurt."

"And I don't want *you* to be hurt. Whatever's happening, I'm not leaving you."

The green dragon cleared his throat. Sebastian thought he was a male, but he couldn't have cared less right now. He only cared that these dragons were trying to hurt Caven.

"What's happening?" the green dragon asked.

"This is Sebastian. He's a human I saved. He needs a safe place to hide, and I thought the clan would welcome him."

The green dragon stared for a moment. "Why did you help a human?"

"Why I did it doesn't matter. The only thing that does is that someone is after him, trying to kill him, and he needs a safe place to stay." Caven hesitated. "Please. I'm ready to follow you to wherever you want to lock me up, but I need to know Sebastian will be safe."

Caven's words finally penetrated Sebastian's mind. It wasn't the first time he or the green dragon mentioned Caven being locked up. It sounded like he'd somehow escaped, but Sebastian couldn't wrap his mind around any of this. Why had Caven been locked up? Why had he run away, and why was he back?

Well, that question was easy to answer. He was back because he thought it was the only way to help Sebastian.

But why had he been locked up?

Sebastian couldn't believe Caven had hurt someone. He didn't have it in him, and it wasn't the kind of person Caven was. But then, what was happening?

Sebastian was confused.

The green dragon turned his attention to Sebastian. "My name is Morven," he said.

Sebastian nodded, but he didn't let go of Caven. If Caven was going to be locked up, then Sebastian would go with him. "I'm Sebastian."

"I know. Do you think you can let go of Caven?"

Sebastian narrowed his eyes. "Are you going to take him away if I do?"

"We have to."

"Then no. I'm not letting him go. If you're going to lock him up, you'll have to lock me up, too."

Caven's arm around Sebastian tightened. "You shouldn't do this," Caven murmured. His gaze flickered to Morven, but it quickly moved back to Sebastian. "Morven will make sure you're safe. You should go with him."

"Nope."

"Sebastian, don't be stubborn."

Sebastian glared at Caven. "You've known me for days. Do you think I'm going to dump your ass when I don't know what's going on? You told me I'd be safe here, and I believed you."

"You *are* safe. No one is going to hurt you." Caven sounded a little desperate, as if he needed Sebastian to let go.

He was stubborn, but Sebastian was even more so, and he wasn't going anywhere until he had an explanation.

And it'd better be a good one.

He didn't care what Caven had done. What he cared about were Caven's actions, and they spoke loudly. Caven could have easily ignored what was happening to Sebastian and walked away. Instead, he'd saved Sebastian from Patrick O'Neill, and then he'd taken him away to a place where Sebastian would be safe. If it weren't for him, Sebastian would already be dead.

"But will they hurt *you*?" Sebastian asked, already knowing the answer.

That was why he wasn't letting go.

Caven didn't know how to answer Sebastian's question. He wanted to tell him that they wouldn't hurt him, but he couldn't be sure. They hadn't hurt him the first time around, but many things had happened since then. He'd escaped, and he'd come back. Unfortunately, there was no way for him to know what was about to happen.

But he still needed to keep Sebastian safe.

"You don't understand," he murmured, trying to get Sebastian to let go. "What happens to me doesn't matter. We're here for you, not for me."

But Sebastian shook his head. "I don't care. I don't trust people who might hurt you to keep me safe."

"They won't do anything to you."

Sebastian looked skeptical, so Caven turned his attention back to Morven. "Please. Don't hurt him."

Morven looked offended. "We would never hurt someone without reason. Sebastian hasn't done anything to the clan or us, so why would we hurt him?"

Caven had heard Morven's words, including those he hadn't said. Sebastian hadn't done anything to the clan, but Caven had. They wouldn't hurt Sebastian, but they might hurt him.

Honestly, he'd expected it. They needed to find out what he'd been up to since he'd run away, and they'd use whatever technique was needed to get answers. The Ogorth clan didn't usually torture, but they just might when it came to Caven. There was no love lost for him in the clan, and if he didn't answer their questions, they'd have to find another way to get what they needed.

"Will you hurt Caven?" Sebastian asked.

Morven stared at him. He didn't say anything, but Sebastian assumed that was his answer.

"I knew it," he said. "I won't allow you to hurt him. He's been nice to me, and he saved my life. How can you people be so hard on him?"

Sebastian was going to ruin any chance he had of having a safe place with the Ogorth clan if he continued talking and defending Caven. Caven had to act, and the only way he knew how to shut up Sebastian was to kiss him. Since that wouldn't be possible here, he slapped a hand against Sebastian's mouth instead.

Sebastian's eyes bugged and he tried to push Caven's hand away, but Caven was stronger, and he was doing it for Sebastian.

"He won't be a problem for the clan," Caven said, looking back at Morven.

To his surprise, Morven seemed amused. "Won't he? Because to me, he looks kind of problematic. He's mouthy."

"He doesn't know," Caven whispered. "I haven't had the opportunity to tell him."

Morven's expression turned serious again. "Haven't you? Because I know how long the trip is from the closest city to here."

"What difference would it have made? I didn't want him to be afraid of me, and he needed me."

Sebastian licked Caven's palm. Caven was so surprised that he jerked his hand away and stared at Sebastian with wide eyes. "What did you do that for?"

Sebastian glared at him. "You will *not* shut me up. If I want to speak, I'll speak, and I don't care what happens to me."

"I brought you here so you'd be safe. Why would you want to ruin your chances of that happening?"

Sebastian was still holding onto Caven, and he wasn't showing signs that he'd let go. That didn't stop him from glaring and scowling and telling Caven exactly what he thought. "I'll ruin my chances to be safe if it means you're safe, too. I don't care what's going on. *You saved my life.* You brought me here, kept me safe and took care of me during the trip. Do you really think I'll abandon you?" He leaned closer, staring Caven in the eyes. "Do you really think I'd abandon you after what happened between us?"

Caven looked away. He had to before he did something stupid. Unfortunately, his gaze crossed with Morven's, who'd heard everything. Morven arched a brow in a silent question, but Caven couldn't answer.

It wasn't that he didn't want people to find out what had happened between him and Sebastian. It was just that he fully expected to be locked up by the end of the day, probably sooner, and it would be better for Sebastian to put some space between them. People knowing Sebastian and Caven had been together would only make Sebastian's life with the clan harder.

"Let me make a phone call," Morven said.

Caven nodded and swallowed. He knew who Morven was about to call, and he watched as the dragon stepped away and reached for the pouch around his neck. Since dragons didn't wear clothes, they had to find other ways to carry their personal objects. Usually, it was in a pouch around their neck or waist. The neck made more sense, because they could shift without a problem and without losing their cell phones if the cord was long enough.

"There's another reason I licked you," Sebastian whispered as he watched Morven.

"What other reason could there be?"

"Well, there's a saying amongst us humans. If you lick it, it's yours."

Caven stared. What was Sebastian talking about? Did Caven even want to know?

He wasn't sure. Humans were strange, and if Caven and Sebastian were in any other situation, Caven would demand an explanation. Instead, he nodded and pressed his lips together.

When he turned, it was to find Hogan staring at them. He didn't look as angry as before, but rather, curious. It was a big difference from the way Hogan had been before. Meeting Cain and falling in love with him had somehow softened Hogan. He'd still be fierce if someone threatened his mate or their child, but he was more relaxed in the other aspects of his life.

He'd always been an angry dragon, and his calmness in this situation made Caven uneasy. He'd fully expected Hogan to growl at him, grab him, and drag him back to his cell. He wouldn't have cared as long as Sebastian was safe. But of course, Sebastian had to complicate things, step in and try to protect Caven. He was the only person who'd ever done that, and it touched something in Caven, but wanting someone to protect him wasn't enough for Caven to want Sebastian to ruin this chance at a safe life.

Caven had to keep in mind that his cousin wanted the clan to have more humans. She wished for the dragons in the Ogorth clan to get to know humans, share their lives with them, and show everyone that it could be done. It had worked incredibly well so far, and Caven wondered if Sebastian would meet someone else once he was gone. It would make sense for him to. He was young, and he shouldn't be alone if that wasn't what he wanted.

But it hurt. Over just a few days, Caven had come to care for Sebastian. He didn't want Sebastian to be with anyone but him, although he wouldn't have a say in it once he was back in his cell. It would be good for Sebastian to meet other dragons and fall in love with one of them. There were many deserving dragons in the clan, and they could all keep Sebastian safe. Once Caven was out of the picture, Sebastian could have a good life.

But even knowing all of that, Caven's heart was breaking.

Sebastian still had no idea what was happening, and he didn't care. If these people thought they were going to hurt Caven, they'd better rethink their plans.

He was terrified. He'd only ever met one dragon before, and it was Caven. He might have always been fascinated by dragons and disgusted by the way humans hunted and killed them, but he hadn't known any dragons. Hell, he'd fully believed dragons were animals until recently.

And now, here he was, wrapped around a dragon shifter, facing down more dragon shifters. He stood on top of a *palace* full of other dragons.

He had no idea what to do beyond protecting Caven. He didn't care much what happened to him, although he hoped it would be painless.

He eyed the black dragon still staring at them.

Okay, so maybe it wouldn't be painless. That dragon looked like he could kill Sebastian without breaking a sweat, and he probably could. But that wouldn't be enough for Sebastian to step away. After what Caven had done for him, after bringing Sebastian here even though it was clear he wasn't welcome, Sebastian was ready to do anything to keep Caven safe.

He just wished someone would give him an explanation.

Thankfully, Morven hung up his phone and moved back toward them. Sebastian suspected he'd called whoever was in charge, which was a queen, from what he remembered. Caven had mentioned her a few times, but he hadn't gone into details. Sebastian prayed she was a good ruler and that she'd give both him and Caven a chance.

A niggle at the back of his mind made him wonder what Caven had done to be locked up and to have dragons hate him so clearly, but now wasn't the time to think about that. He knew Caven. He'd watched him over the past few days, and whatever had happened in the past, Caven wasn't a bad person. He couldn't be, because he'd have abandoned Sebastian to his fate if he had been.

"The two of you, follow me," Morven ordered.

Sebastian and Caven exchanged a glance. Caven turned his attention back to Morven and nodded, but Sebastian wanted more.

"Where are you taking us?" he asked Morven.

"You have to let me go so I can walk," Caven whispered.

He wasn't wrong, so Sebastian unwrapped himself from around Caven. He didn't let go of him entirely, though. He grabbed one of Caven's arms and hung onto it with both of his, glaring at Morven and whoever else looked at them. He didn't care what they thought of him. He'd keep Caven safe even if it killed him, although he hoped that wouldn't happen. He was here because he wanted to live, after all.

"Do you always ask so many questions?" Morven asked. He didn't look angry but rather curious.

"I ask as many questions as I need to know what's happening."

Morven nodded. "I suppose that makes sense. My mate

had a lot of questions in the beginning, too."

Sebastian was curious. "What about your mate?"

Morven turned and started walking. Sebastian had to rush to keep up with Caven, who followed Morven. The guards around them parted, letting Morven through. When Sebastian turned, he wasn't surprised to see the black dragon was behind them. He and Caven were caged in, although leaving all these other dragons behind was a relief. Apparently, only Morven and the black dragon would walk them wherever they were going.

"He had many questions when he first arrived here, too," Morven eventually said. He looked hesitant, possibly to talk about his mate.

"Why?" Sebastian asked.

"Because he's human, like you. I'm sure you'll meet him soon."

So Morven was with one of the two humans who lived with the clan. Sebastian wasn't sure whether or not to be surprised. Maybe it explained why Morven hadn't decided to get rid of him on sight. He was used to dealing with humans.

Sebastian opened his mouth to ask more questions, but just then, he also stepped off the platform where he and Caven had landed through a big opening in the mountain wall. The simple polished stone gave way to carpets and artworks on the walls.

Sebastian looked around with wide eyes. He'd seen the palace from a distance, but he couldn't have imagined it would be like this. For one, it was much bigger than he could ever have thought. He supposed it made sense, since most of the people living here were dragons.

They walked past some of them in their dragon form, and Sebastian did his best not to stare. He didn't want to be rude, especially if he was going to live here.

But he couldn't be sure of that just yet.

He leaned closer to Caven. "Where are we going?"

Caven shook his head. "Just be quiet. Agree to whatever is about to happen."

"You mean, agree to let you go."

Caven didn't look at Sebastian but instead kept his focus straight ahead. "We're here for you," he whispered. "I brought you to the clan so they'd keep you safe. It won't work if you don't agree to their terms."

"I don't care about that if it means you're not with me. It's us against the world, right?"

Maybe that was a bit dramatic, considering they'd only known each other a few days, but Sebastian didn't care. He and Caven had spent all their time together in those few days. They'd only had one thing to do, and it was talking. Sebastian hadn't told Caven about his entire life, just like Caven hadn't, but they knew each other.

Sebastian wasn't doing anything if Caven wasn't with him.

They continued walking down hallways and turning corners. Sebastian almost tripped when they reached what looked to be a central room. It was massive and open in the center. Sebastian didn't understand why until he saw a dragon rise from somewhere at the bottom.

Around the room ran a set of stairs. They took it, and Sebastian looked down, even though there was no railing. He swallowed when he saw how high up he and the others were. This was a staircase, and since dragons lived in this palace, the center was empty so they could fly up and down. If Sebastian fell, though, he'd break his neck, and that was if he was lucky.

They went down several floors, then walked into yet another hallway. Things were even more luxurious here, if that was even possible. They also passed more dragons, and all of them seemed curious about Sebastian. One even stumbled, they were so busy staring at Sebastian.

Even though Sebastian was in awe of so many dragons, he pressed closer to Caven. It was intimidating to have so many eyes on him, especially the eyes of people who could kill him with barely a thought.

Caven pulled Sebastian closer. "No one here will hurt you."

"That you know of, but your clan is bigger than I expected. I doubt you're friends with everyone."

"I don't really have friends."

Sebastian frowned. That was sad. "I'm your friend."

"For now," Caven agreed.

Sebastian wanted to tell him that would never change and that he'd always be his friend, but he didn't dare. He had no idea what was in Caven's past and what he'd done, and while he didn't want to find out, he suspected that sooner rather than later, he would. He had no idea how he'd react then, but he didn't want to make promises he couldn't keep, especially not to Caven.

They paused in front of a wide set of doors. They were made of wood and sculpted with images of dragons, both in their animal form and in their human form.

Morven didn't hesitate. He briefly knocked, then pushed open one of the doors. The guards standing in the hallway nodded at him, and they didn't try to stop him. Clearly, he was expected.

Caven sucked in a breath, but he didn't hesitate to follow Morven through. Since Sebastian was still clinging to him, he had no choice but to go along.

They stepped into what looked like a throne room. It was similar to throne rooms Sebastian had seen in fantasy movies, so he knew what to expect when he and Caven faced the dragon in human form sitting on the throne.

This had to be the queen Caven had told Sebastian about.

CHAPTER SEVEN

Ita was staring at Sebastian as if he were a curious insect. If Caven hadn't known her, he would have wondered if she was about to order Sebastian to be hurt. He wanted to beg her to keep Sebastian safe, but instead, he pressed his lips together and waited for her to speak.

"Welcome," she said, still staring at Sebastian. "I'm Queen Ita."

Sebastian nervously chuckled. "I guessed that. Should I bow?"

The queen smiled. "You don't need to."

"Well, thank you. I'm Sebastian."

"Morven told me. He told me many things, but if you don't mind, I'd like to hear them from you."

Sebastian's hold on Caven's arm tightened. Caven wanted to reassure Sebastian that no one here would hurt him, so he patted his hand. Sebastian gave him a grateful smile, and Caven smiled back.

When they both turned back to the queen, Caven didn't miss how she looked from him to Sebastian. He had no doubt she had questions and that she was about to ask them.

"This is the Ogorth clan's home, Sebastian," she said. "Humans are welcome here, but I'd like to know more about your presence with us."

Sebastian nodded. "I saw something. A man killed a woman. I wanted to stop him, but he killed her before I could, and after she was dead, there was nothing I could do for her. I hid, but he saw me, and he came after me. He found me even after I ran, and he was about to kill me so I wouldn't tell any-one what he'd done."

"I'm sorry you had to go through that," the queen said when Sebastian didn't continue.

Sebastian nodded curtly. "Thank you. I thought for sure I'd die, but that's when Caven stepped in. He pulled Patrick, the guy trying to kill me, off me. He grabbed me and flew me away, and when Patrick said he knew where I lived, Caven offered to take me somewhere safe."

The queen looked at Caven. "And this is somewhere safe for you?" she asked him.

Caven cleared his throat. "I couldn't think of a safer place for Sebastian. Please, allow him to stay. Protect Sebastian and make sure that man doesn't hurt him." Caven knew it wasn't that easy, but it could be. It would have to be, for Sebastian.

"You brought him here, even after everything that hap-pened. You knew we would likely lock you up again, yet here you are. I find that hard to believe."

"I will gladly let you lock me up if it means Sebastian is safe." The words tasted like ashes, but Caven was more than happy to say them. Right now, nothing mattered more to him than Sebastian's safety.

"I have to admit I find surprising how much you care about a human. Is it because he's the father of your baby?"

The world stopped. Caven had heard the words, but his brain couldn't make sense of them.

It just wasn't possible.

He stared at his cousin for what felt like an eternity. She waited, seemingly content to give Caven time to understand what she was saying. She still didn't say anything when Caven slowly lowered his head to look at his stomach.

The pregnancy line was visible to anyone who looked at him.

Caven's head spun. He might have fallen if Sebastian

hadn't been there, holding him up. He stepped in front of Caven, a frown marring his beautiful face.

"Are you okay?" he asked.

Caven wasn't sure he could answer or if he was okay. He wasn't sure of anything.

How could this have happened?

He knew how it had happened. He and Sebastian had sex, and Sebastian impregnated him. He hadn't even realized he was fertile. He hadn't kept up with the signs because it hadn't mattered. Caven had left his life behind, and he'd had no intention of being with anyone, so he wouldn't get pregnant.

Except, he was.

"Caven?" Sebastian sounded like he was freaking out, and Caven didn't blame him. He didn't know both male and female dragons could carry a child. He hadn't known it was a possibility when they'd been together, and now, Caven would have to tell him.

He was carrying Sebastian's child.

Would the egg be taken from him when he laid it? Ita would probably give it to Sebastian to raise, and Caven would be stuck in his cell and not allowed to know his child. He'd never thought about having children, sure that whoever he married would do so for him, but now that he knew, he couldn't give up the baby.

He pressed a hand against his stomach. He was pregnant, and it should have been a blessing. It was, in a way, but it would also tear Caven's heart out when the child was taken from him.

"You're freaking me out, and I don't react well when I'm freaking out," Sebastian said.

But Caven didn't know what to tell him. He could do nothing but stare at his stomach, at the line there.

A hand on his arm made him jerk away. He looked up to see his cousin standing there, smiling at him. His brain didn't understand what was happening or why Ita seemed almost happy.

"Why don't you sit down?" she said.

Caven nodded, unable to say anything. He allowed her to guide him toward the corner of the room, where a small sitting area was hidden behind curtains. It was under a window, and Caven could smell the forest with it open. It was soothing, because to him it was home, but the turmoil was still very much present in his mind.

He was pregnant.

He looked at the people around him. Thankfully, only Morven and Hogan were present. They'd be the only ones to know Caven was pregnant, and by a human to boot. Caven had no way to know if they'd tell anyone, but he supposed it didn't matter. His father would find out, and he'd be the angriest Caven had ever seen him.

Although Caven supposed he wouldn't actually see his father that angry. He'd be behind bars, and his father wouldn't visit. He hadn't last time.

His knees wobbled as he sat on one of the couches. Sebastian had never let him go, and he sat next to him. He leaned against Caven, rubbing his back, his expression an angry frown.

"What did you do to him?" Sebastian demanded to know.

Ita raised her hands. "I noticed a line on his stomach, and I asked him about the baby."

The frown was still firmly stuck on Sebastian's face. "The line on his stomach? It was there last night, too." He peered at Caven. "Although it was different. It wasn't as visible, I guess."

If Sebastian was about to find out he'd gotten Caven pregnant, Caven should be the one to tell him. He looked at his cousin. He didn't want to do this here. He wanted Sebastian to have time and space to wrap his mind around what it meant for him, and even more so, he wanted them to be alone in case Sebastian was disgusted with what had happened. He hadn't known this was a possibility, and Caven needed him to have the opportunity to step away if he wasn't ready for a child.

If that was what Sebastian wanted, Caven would have to fight so the baby wouldn't be given to his parents. That meant he'd have to explain to his cousin what his father had done and what he was still doing, and while he wasn't looking forward to it, maybe it was time to do just that.

Ita cleared her throat. "It's obvious this was a surprise to you, and while I'm curious as to what happened, I won't ask questions just yet. If either of you ever wants to tell me, I'll be available to listen. In the meantime, considering the circumstances, I won't put you back in your cell, Caven."

Caven stared. He didn't know what to say or how to thank his cousin. His first instinct was to not trust what she was saying, but he forced himself to ignore it. His first instinct was his father talking, and his father was the last person Caven should be listening to. If he found out Caven was pregnant with Sebastian's baby, he'd demand Caven get rid of it. He would never stand for a half-human grandchild, and he'd expect Caven to go along with what he wanted.

For the first time, Caven wouldn't do it. Whatever happened, whatever his father or anyone else wanted, Caven was keeping his baby. The only ones who could make decisions for the baby were him and Sebastian.

But Sebastian still didn't understand what was happening.

Sebastian wanted to scream and demand answers, but what the queen was saying was important. Caven had expected her to stick him back into his cell, but instead, she was doing the opposite.

"Of course, there will be conditions," she continued.

Caven lightly bowed his head. "Whatever you want," he murmured.

"I'd like for you to tell me what happened to you and why you left. I believe I know the reason behind that, but something happened to you while you were gone. You changed much more than I thought was possible. That leads me to believe there was more to what I could see of you before, and I feel I need to know things I should have realized before."

"I'll tell you whatever you want to know."

The queen nodded. "Good. So, we'll have meetings. You'll put everything on the table, no matter how you feel about it or what you think my reaction will be. You'll also be in charge of Sebastian. I'll allow him to stay with the clan, since, as you know, I want more humans to live with us. You'll show him around, explain the rules of living at the palace, and tell him everything he needs to know."

"So I can stay?" Sebastian asked.

The queen's smile was gentle. "I would never turn you away, especially since you're in danger. We can talk more about your situation later, but for now, I think both you and Caven need some time to rest and relax. As soon as this meeting is over, you'll be shown to Caven's rooms."

"Not my rooms with my parents," Caven snapped. "I apologize for my tone, but I can't be with them."

He pressed a hand to his stomach again, and Sebastian couldn't look away. If he twisted his head just right, he could see the line on Caven's stomach. It had been there last night when they'd made love, but he hadn't realized it was special. It had been visible since the first time he'd met Caven, and he'd thought it was normal.

But it was different now. It was thicker and darker, much more obvious than it had been before.

And had the queen been talking about a baby?

Sebastian was confused, but he'd heard her ask if he was the father of Caven's baby. Was that what that line meant? Could male dragons become pregnant? And could it happen so fast? He and Caven had made love yesterday evening after they'd woken up. They'd reached the palace after flying for more than twelve hours, which had felt like forever, but it wasn't, especially when talking about pregnancy.

Sebastian wanted answers, but since everything seemed to be all right, he'd get them later. Right now, he was more worried about himself and Caven being allowed to stay with the clan and about Caven's health. He could freak out about possibly becoming a father of a dragon-human hybrid later.

The queen nodded. "I'm not surprised to hear that, and we'll find you another set of rooms. I'll make sure they're big enough for your family."

"Thank you."

Caven looked like he might be about to cry, and Sebastian pressed closer to him. Caven gave him a wobbly smile, and Sebastian couldn't avoid smiling back. He was always smiling when it came to Caven.

But now he was even more puzzled about this entire situation. Caven didn't want to stay with his parents. Clearly, he wasn't looking forward to seeing them again, which made Sebastian wonder. Did Caven have a bad relationship with his parents?

Sebastian supposed dragons were like any other species. His aunt and uncle had disowned his cousin because he was gay. Was Caven afraid his parents would do the same when they found out he was pregnant?

Sebastian needed to find out more about dragons and their culture. He was completely lost, and he disliked feeling that way.

"And I expect you to talk to the people you hurt and apologize for what you've done. It will be their decision whether or not to forgive you, but if you're going to be staying with the clan and become a productive part of it again, this is one condition I won't go back on."

Caven had paled before, but now, his skin blanched even more. Sebastian squeezed one of his hands, wanting to be close to him and help him but not knowing how to do so. His support seemed to be enough, though, because Caven nodded.

"I'll apologize to everyone I hurt if they allow me to, and I'll explain why I did what I did."

"You will eventually, but first, *I* want to hear that story."

"I can tell you now."

"No. You've been traveling for days, and in your condition, you need rest. You probably pushed yourself more than you should have, since you didn't know you were expecting." She looked at Morven. "Can you find Ruy for me? Ask him to give Caven a set of rooms in my private wing."

Morven's eyes widened, but he nodded. "I'll go now," he said.

"Thank you." She turned her attention back to Caven and Sebastian. "I'm not putting you in my wing to keep an eye on you, but rather, to make sure you're all right. Besides, Caven is my cousin. My family belongs in my wing of the palace."

Sebastian agreed with that, but it was clear her demand meant something. Caven leaned forward, staring at her.

"I don't understand," he said.

"I don't, either. I always wondered why you did what you did, and even more so after the meetings with the other clans. Don't think I didn't see how you protected the Ogorth clan. Between that, the fact that you're here with a human mate, and your reaction to going back to your parents, I suspect there's a lot I don't know about your situation. I don't like that you didn't feel you could come to me, and I intend to change that. It doesn't erase what you've done, and you'll have to atone, but I'm ready to give you a chance."

Caven looked down. He looked like he might be about to cry, but it was clear he didn't want his cousin to see it.

Man, families were complicated.

Sebastian had thought his was bad between his aunt and uncle kicking his cousin out and his mother dying, but they had nothing on dragon families.

Which reminded him that he needed to call Christian.

"You won't regret it," Caven promised.

"I don't think I will, no," the queen agreed.

Morven reappeared, interrupting the conversation. He wasn't alone, and Sebastian stared at the dragon walking behind him. He'd seen many dragons since he'd entered the palace, but this dragon had to be the prettiest yet. Like every other dragon in their human form, he had claws on his fingers and toes and patches of his skin were scaly and colorful. Those parts of his skin, his hair, and his eyes were a light pastel orange. He looked like a sunrise or maybe a sunset, and seeing him made Sebastian smile for some reason. There was no way someone who looked like that wasn't nice, right?

"Your Majesty," the dragon said.

Sebastian squinted, trying to understand if the dragon was male or female. He supposed it didn't matter, but as a human, he was used to being able to understand that on sight. With dragons, it was nearly impossible. Female dragons like the queen had breasts, but they weren't big, and they could be confused with pectorals. It made the identification harder, but while Sebastian was curious, he wasn't about to ask. If this dragon wanted to tell him, they would. Still, if Sebastian had to guess, he'd say he was in front of a male dragon.

"I need your help, Ruy."

"Whatever you need, your Majesty."

If this was the dragon the queen had mentioned earlier, he was male because, she'd used male pronouns when she talked of him.

"As you can see, my cousin is back. He needs a set of rooms to settle in with his family, and I want him to be in my wing."

Ruy's gaze snapped up. "Your Majesty?"

"You heard me. Make sure to leave enough space between us that we don't bother each other, but I want Caven and his family close. I believe the problems started when Caven's family moved out of the royal wing, and I intend to fix that."

Sebastian had even more questions now, but they could wait. It looked like the queen would allow both him and Caven to stay at the palace, and she was going so far as to give them rooms close to her. That meant Sebastian and Caven were safe, and that was all that mattered.

Caven was still confused and bewildered as he followed Ruy down the hallway. Sebastian clung to his hand, seemingly planning on never letting go, and Morven walked next to them. He'd opened his mouth a few times as if he was about to ask a question, but he'd apparently thought better of it and had closed it every time.

Good. Caven had no idea what Morven wanted to ask, but he suspected he wouldn't have been able to answer.

But the silence was tense and awkward. Ruy was babbling about something Caven didn't care about, filling the silence like he always did. Sebastian was looking around, his eyes wide as he took in the royal wing of the palace.

This was the wing where the royal family lived. Once, it had meant the king or queen and their consort, their children, their brothers and sisters, their parents, and everyone's families. But when Ita's father had passed and she'd taken his place on the throne, Caven's father had decided to move out. Everyone knew it was because he didn't respect his niece as the queen, and that had been a sure way to let her know. It had been rude and unheard of, and Caven was kind of glad that his cousin was bringing back the tradition.

But his father would be pissed. Caven supposed he could add it to the long list of reasons his father would be angry at him and possibly try to kill him.

Maybe that was one more reason his cousin was keeping him close. She knew how his father would react, and she probably suspected that he had a lot to do with what Caven had done.

Caven had wanted the opportunity to atone, and Ita was giving him just that.

"You'll be several hallways away from the queen," Ruy said as he stopped in front of a door.

Caven remembered the royal wing from when he was a child. He and his family hadn't lived in the rooms where Ruy was putting him and Sebastian, thankfully. Caven didn't have good memories of those rooms.

"As I'm sure you remember, the entire wing is protected by guards," Ruy continued. "You'll be safer here than you could be anywhere else in the palace. There will be servants at your disposal, although I hope you'll treat them well."

Caven winced. He knew his reputation, but he hadn't expected to have to face it. Now, he would have to, and since Ruy was here, he might as well start with him. "I apologize for anything I said in the past that was rude," he said formally.

Ruy blinked at him. "I suppose I accept your apology."

"You *suppose* you do?"

"I don't understand why the queen is doing this, but it's not my place to understand it. I'm sure she has her reasons, and since she seems to trust you enough to have you live close to her, then I trust you, too." He leaned forward. "But I'll be keeping an eye on you. I don't care that you came here with a human mate or that you're pregnant. I'll find out if this is a ruse, and you'll pay for it."

"It isn't," Caven promised. "Sebastian and I just want to be able to live in peace."

Ruy stared for a moment, then nodded. "Good. I'll have servants pick up your things at your parents' and bring them here. I'm sure you'll be more comfortable with things that are familiar to you."

"Thank you." Caven didn't know what else to say. He hadn't expected any of this to happen, and he needed some time to digest all of it.

Ruy nodded curtly, turned around, and walked down the hallway. He was already tapping on the tablet that never seemed to leave his hand, and Caven suspected he'd get his things sooner rather than later. He wasn't sure how he felt about that. They were his, but they felt like they belonged to another life and another Caven.

"I want to congratulate you on the baby," Morven said.

Caven had almost forgotten he was still there. He tensed, unsure how to take Morven's words.

"Caven, if you have any questions or worries, I want you to know you can come to me. Considering my history and what happened between Sheldon and I, and of course, our daughter, I can understand better than anyone what you're going through."

Because he was the only one in the clan who had a child with a human.

Thankfully, Sheldon and Morven's daughter was perfectly fine. It gave Caven hope that his and Sebastian's baby would be okay, too.

"Thank you," he croaked.

"Okay, I *need* to know what you're talking about," Sebastian suddenly said.

He'd been mostly silent until now, but he seemed to have reached the end of his patience.

Morven eyed him. "You still don't understand?"

"I think I do, but I'm not sure, and it's driving me nuts. Can you just explain in plain words? I don't want to misunderstand and do something I shouldn't."

"Male dragons can carry eggs," Caven said. It was his place to tell Sebastian about this.

"When you say carry eggs, what do you mean?" Sebastian asked.

Caven had researched human sexuality and reproduction, so he knew it was different from how dragons worked. "We don't give birth to live babies. We lay eggs, and eventually, they hatch, and the baby is born. Both male and female dragons can carry the eggs. We can both get pregnant, which rarely happens, because we're not a very fertile race." He pressed a hand to his stomach. "When we're fertile, a line appears on our stomach, from our belly button to our pouch. Those are the only times we can get pregnant. I didn't realize it was that time for me, but then, I was distracted. Unfortunately, it means that when we were together in the forest, we created a life. We're going to be parents."

Sebastian opened his mouth, but the only thing that came out of it was a croak. His eyes were so wide that Caven wouldn't have been surprised if they'd popped out of their sockets. Sebastian was in shock.

Morven cleared his throat. "I'll leave you to it. I'm sure you both need time to wrap your mind around what happened." He turned to Sebastian. "When you're ready, I'll introduce you to my mate. He's been in your position. I didn't realize I was fertile, either, which is how I ended up pregnant."

"How is this possible?" Sebastian asked. He sounded lost.

"Take some time. You're safe here, and you don't have to worry that someone will attack you. Welcome to the clan, Sebastian."

With that, Morven left. It was kind of surprising, because

Caven hadn't expected any of this to happen, but he wanted more time with Sebastian. The problem was that he had no idea what Sebastian wanted.

Would he want to live with Caven and the baby? Would he want to be a father?

And those questions didn't even consider the rest of the clan. Caven's father would kill him for having a child with someone useless to their cause, especially because that someone was human. Caven would have to deal with him, and soon.

But first, he'd take care of Sebastian. It was the least he could do for the human he was falling in love with.

"Why don't we go inside?" he suggested.

Sebastian nodded, but as Caven opened the door to step into what was now their home, Sebastian grabbed Caven's wrist. "I'm not dreaming any of this, am I? You and I are really having a baby together?"

Caven nodded. "I'm sorry if this isn't what you wanted. There are ways for me not to be pregnant anymore, but unless you're absolutely against you and I having a child, I'd like to have this baby, even if you want nothing to do with them. Children are precious to dragons because of how rare pregnancies are." And this child was precious to Caven in a way he hadn't expected.

Sebastian scowled at him and raised his finger to point at Caven's nose. "Don't you dare say something like that. I'm in shock, and I never thought something like this would happen to me, but it doesn't mean I don't want this baby or that I don't want you. I won't deny it'll take some time for me to wrap my mind around all of this, but we're in it together. I need you to understand that, and that I'm not going anywhere. You and the baby are my family."

Caven found himself beaming without meaning to. He'd been afraid of Sebastian's reaction, but he shouldn't have been. Once again, Sebastian surprised him by being himself.

Caven wouldn't have it any other way. He wouldn't have any of this any other way.

CHAPTER EIGHT

Caven was avoiding his parents. To be fair, he avoided everyone, including Sebastian, although not for the same reasons.

Sebastian had been behaving as if Caven was made of glass since he'd found out Caven was pregnant. For the first two days after they'd arrived at the palace, he'd refused to let Caven leave the rooms they now shared. After that, he'd reluctantly allowed Caven to leave, but he followed him around, as if he was afraid Caven was about to faint. Caven was pretty sure that human women weren't that fragile even when they were pregnant, but no amount of pointing that out had changed Sebastian's mind. Every time Caven said something about it, Sebastian answered that he'd never gotten anyone pregnant, so he wouldn't know how women were during that time, but even if he had, he'd have been just as worried.

But Sebastian wasn't what bothered Caven the most. No, that was the people staring. It was almost enough to convince him that he *should* stay in their rooms.

Caven refused to let the clan intimidate him into locking himself up, especially now that he didn't have a cell anymore. His cousin had welcomed him back, which meant he was a clan member. He had every right to walk the hallways and eat in the dining hall, no matter what he heard some of the other dragons mutter as he walked past.

Every time they insulted him or wondered what he was doing there, he raised his chin higher. Every time they noticed the pregnancy line on his stomach, he did the same. Eventually, they'd stop staring, right?

Caven was fine with just Sebastian by his side. Even though the way Sebastian behaved was slightly annoying at times, it showed that he cared, and right now, he was the only one who cared about Caven at all. Caven knew how precious that was, but even more importantly, he knew how precious *Sebastian* was. Watching him discover things about dragons and the palace, seeing how wide his eyes went and how excited he was, was almost enough for Caven not to regret coming back.

If he hadn't agreed to help Sebastian, he wouldn't be here, back with the clan and pregnant with a human's child. Some days, he wondered if maybe that would have been better. Then Sebastian did something sweet and endearing, and Caven knew he'd done the right thing. There was no going back, and he didn't *want* to go back. He was home, he had Sebastian, and that was what he needed to focus on.

"Are you sure you're up to leaving the room?" Sebastian asked from next to Caven.

They were walking toward the dining hall. Sebastian hadn't asked what Caven had done to be locked up before, and Caven hadn't volunteered the information. Eventually, they'd have to talk about it, and he fully expected Sebastian to be disgusted with what he'd done and leave him, but in the meantime, he'd enjoy the time they had together.

He didn't know what would happen once Sebastian found out. Would he demand to be given their child? Or would they have to find a way to make things work without spending time together? Sometimes that happened, but it was infrequent to have parents separate during a pregnancy. Dragon pregnancies were usually desired and cherished, and though Caven was happy to have a child, it hadn't been planned. Everything around him was a mess, including the life he now shared with Sebastian. He expected something to break at any moment, and he was honestly surprised it hadn't happened yet. He couldn't imagine things would stay this way for much longer. Eventually, someone would tell Sebastian what he'd done, and then Sebastian would leave him.

"Caven?" Sebastian asked.

Caven recognized that tone of voice. If he didn't reassure Sebastian, Sebastian would grab him and drag him back to their rooms.

So Caven forced himself to smile. "I'm fine, and yes, I'm up to going to the dining hall. I already told you that I'm not fragile and that you don't have to protect me just because I'm pregnant."

Sebastian rolled his eyes. "And I already told you I'd behave this way with anyone I'd gotten pregnant. Hell, I'd do it for pregnant people in general. I mean, think about it. Pregnancy is a miracle, isn't it? There has to be a meeting of circumstances, the right time, the right place, and everything. And the pregnancy itself? You're creating a baby. Your body is creating a baby without anyone telling it what to do or how to do it."

"I'm creating an egg," Caven pointed out.

"And that egg will become a baby. Don't try to distract me."

Caven pressed his lips together so he wouldn't laugh. This was one of the reasons he liked spending time with Sebastian so much. He was in awe of the little things Caven was used to and viewed as normal. It could be as big as the pregnancy or as small as one of the decorations carved on the wall. Sebastian saw everything with new eyes, and it was incredible.

The noise level went up, a sure sign they were almost at the dining hall. Caven had to resist the urge to turn around and head back to the rooms he and Sebastian shared. It was his right to be here, amongst the other dragons, but not all clan members agreed. Most of them didn't understand why the queen had allowed him to come back, although they suspected it had to do with Caven's pregnancy.

They weren't wrong. Caven thought that if he hadn't been pregnant, and even more importantly, if he hadn't been with Sebastian, his cousin would have locked him back in his cell without a second thought.

But meeting Sebastian had changed Caven, and it had surprised Ita enough to want to give Caven a second chance. That was one more thing Caven owed Sebastian.

They walked into the dining hall. Sebastian tensed next to Caven, no doubt because he'd heard some of the things the clan members had said over the past couple of days. Caven took his hand and squeezed, silently trying to reassure him. He wasn't sure he managed, but he needed Sebastian to be okay with the dragons who lived with the clan. They were Sebastian's new family, no matter what they said about Caven.

Caven could have sworn most of the dragons in the room stopped talking for a second when they noticed him. He raised his chin high and pulled Sebastian toward the long tables heavy with food. He didn't care if everyone stared or what they thought of him. The only people he cared about were Sebastian and the queen, and they were both glad to have Caven here.

That was all that mattered.

"I don't like how they keep staring at you," Sebastian muttered as they grabbed food.

"Ignore them."

"I would if that one wasn't ogling your ass."

Caven didn't turn around to see who Sebastian was talking about. He was pretty sure Sebastian had misinterpreted whatever was happening, anyway. "They're just surprised," he said.

"Yeah, I can see that. Doesn't mean they have to be rude about it."

Caven couldn't say he disagreed, but he kept that to himself. They found an empty table and sat down, and Caven had every intention of focusing on his food. He looked up, though, and his gaze crossed with Sheldon's.

They were all gathered at a long table at the back of the room. Caven could see Sheldon, Sheldon's brother Blake, and Sheldon's daughter from where he was. She was in her human form and using her hands to eat what was in a bowl in front of her on the table. Sheldon was holding her, and somehow, he managed to avoid her tiny dirty fists every time she waved them around.

The brothers weren't alone. Their respective mates were there, too, along with Hogan, Cain, their son, and the queen's son. It was the first time Caven found all of them together, and he thought back to what his cousin had told him.

He needed to apologize.

He looked down at his plate. He wasn't hungry, anyway. He could do this, then leave, and it would be one less thing to worry about.

He got to his feet. Sebastian was still talking and eating, and he didn't realize what Caven was doing for a few seconds. Caven left him at the table, sure no one would hurt or bother him. He made his way across the hall, his gaze focused on the group in front of him.

Sheldon had been staring at him, and now, he was frowning. He surely expected Caven to do something stupid, which Caven couldn't blame him for. He'd done plenty of stupid things not so long ago.

He paused at the end of their table and cleared his throat. He had to wait a moment for everyone to look at him, and when they did, he opened his mouth. The first thing that came out was a croak, but he quickly managed to get the words out.

He'd been thinking about those words so many times since he'd come back. He'd gotten a speech ready and everything, but he found himself stumbling through it.

"I wanted to apologize for my behavior in the past," he declared. "What I did was horrible and criminal, and I would deserve to be locked in a cell again. I don't know why my cousin thought to give me a second chance, but I'll show you and her that the opportunity won't be wasted. I will protect the Ogorth clan and every single member of it, be they dragon or human."

Having said what he needed to say, Caven nodded and turned. Someone called out for him, but he didn't turn to check who it was. Instead, he stared straight ahead as he left the room.

Sebastian had no idea what was happening, but when Caven rushed out of the room, he scrambled to his feet to follow. He snatched a roll of bread from his plate as he did so just in case Caven was hungry. They could go to the kitchen to get something to eat anytime they wanted, but Sebastian was still intimidated by the clan and the dragons who lived here. He was more comfortable spending time with Caven in their rooms, and the less they left it, the better he felt.

He hadn't told Caven that. Instead, he'd told him that he wanted them to stay in because it was better for Caven's health, considering he was pregnant. It was probably ridiculous, but Sebastian did feel like what was happening to Caven's body was a miracle, one he'd never expected to experience.

He'd never thought he'd have kids. It wasn't because he was gay, but rather because he couldn't imagine himself in a stable relationship and with children. He still couldn't many days, but he supposed it would happen once the baby was born.

Someone stepped in his path, making him stumble. He looked up to find a gray dragon in their human form staring at him. He gave them a tight smile, then tried to walk around them, but they sidestep him, blocking him again.

"How can you be with him?" they demanded to know.

Sebastian swallowed. He reminded himself that no one would hurt him, no matter what they said. The queen had promised, and he believed her. If someone did try to do something to him, she'd punish them.

"I'm sorry, I have something to do."

"Yeah, with that asshole. How can you be okay with what he did?"

Sebastian raised his hands. "I have no idea what he did, but it doesn't change the fact that he and I are having a child."

The dragon's eyes narrowed. "He had Sheldon and Blake attacked when they first arrived. He tried to push his cousin off the throne to take her place. When Cain ran away from his clan because they wanted to take his baby, Caven kidnapped him and was about to give him back. He would have if he hadn't been arrested."

Sebastian felt faint. He couldn't look away from the dragon, but his brain wasn't connecting. He'd heard the words, and knew what they meant, but he couldn't fit the image the dragon had created of Caven with what he knew of the dragon he was falling in love with.

Had Caven really done those things?

The dragon leaned closer. "He's rotten to the core, and that will never change. It doesn't matter that he let a human impregnate him. It doesn't change who he is."

"That's enough," a strong voice snapped.

The dragon startled and jumped away from Sebastian. Sebastian was grateful, but before he could take advantage of the opportunity and run away, a hand clasped his shoulder.

"Leave Sebastian alone," the voice added.

Sebastian was pretty sure he recognized it as Morven's, and he was relieved to see he was right when he turned his head to find the green dragon standing behind him.

"I was just telling him what Caven did," the gray dragon said.

"It's not your place to tell him."

"He should know who he's with, though."

"Maybe so, but again, it's not your place to make that decision."

The gray dragon huffed, but they finally stepped away. Sebastian waited until they were sitting down to relax, and when he did, he turned his attention to Morven. "Thank you."

Morven smiled. "Don't worry about it. And I'm sorry about what just happened."

"Don't be. It's clear Caven and I need to have a conversation about this, but I think we've both been afraid to have it."

Morven nodded. "It makes sense."

Sebastian hesitated, then decided he might as well ask. "Is what the dragon said true?"

Morven stared at him for a moment. Sebastian held his breath, hoping Morven was about to say it wasn't, but instead, Morven nodded. "I'm sorry, but it is. Caven did have some of his friends attack Blake and Sheldon. Luckily, they weren't hurt, but Caven was never happy to have them with the clan."

"What about Cain?"

Morven sighed. "That was true, too. Cain's old clan took the eggs from their parents. They raised the eggs all together away from the rest of the clan, and the children never got to find out who their parents where. Cain didn't want that to happen to his child, so he ran away. When his clan found out where he was, they demanded we hand him back, but we refused. I'm not sure why Caven kidnapped Cain and tried to give him back, mostly because I've never talked to Caven about it. He was arrested and locked up when that happened."

Sebastian was about to throw up. He looked around, hoping not to do it all over Morven, but since he didn't want to make a fool of himself, he screwed his eyes shut and breathed.

Morven's hand was still on his shoulder, strong and gentle, anchoring Sebastian in the moment. He focused on that rather than on his stomach. "Thank you for telling me."

Morven hesitated. "It wasn't that dragon's place to tell you, just like it wasn't mine. You need to talk to Caven."

"Oh, I will."

"But he's changed. I know you can't see it, because you only met him recently, but I truly believe he's not the Caven he was before. It's strange to say that, because I never liked him, but I can't deny what's in front of me. I think the queen is right and that there was a reason Caven behaved the way he did. We won't find out until we talk to him, which will happen soon. In the meantime, you should talk to him. Give him a chance to explain."

Sebastian nodded, although he wasn't sure how he'd manage that.

He wanted to give Caven a chance. He didn't want to believe that the Caven he'd fallen in love with was the same who'd kidnapped a man who just had a baby. He wouldn't find out what truly happened until they had that conversation, so he stepped away from Morven.

He could feel everyone staring at him as he left the room, but he didn't care. They were about to have the conversation they should have had a while ago.

He knew where to find Caven. He always retreated to their rooms once he was done eating, and today wasn't any different. When Sebastian walked in, it was to find Caven standing by one of the windows, looking outside. He didn't turn when he heard Sebastian because he already knew it could only be him. They were the only two people allowed in their rooms.

"We need to talk," Sebastian said.

Caven nodded but didn't turn to him. "I agree. You heard me apologize?"

"No, but I heard what one of the dragons who was eating had to say about you. They told me that you attacked Blake and Sheldon and that you kidnapped Cain and tried to hand him over to his old clan."

Sebastian couldn't see Caven's expression, and he wanted to. He needed to know Caven truly had changed. So, he moved until he was standing next to Caven. He leaned his shoulder against the wall by the window, staring at the man he loved.

"Is it true?" he asked.

Caven was still staring outside. "It is. I did all of that and more."

"Why?"

"Because I was trying to save the clan."

"That doesn't make sense."

"But it does. All my life, my father told me that I was supposed to take his brother's place on the throne when he died. It's what my father raised me to be. I didn't have friends because I wasn't supposed to waste time on them. I needed allies, people who would obey my orders, but never friends. I couldn't care about anyone, including family. My only goal had to be to get on the throne and keep the clan safe. So that's what I did. When the first human arrived, my father told me he was a threat to everything the clan had built until now. His presence would bring other humans, and he was right. Sheldon arrived soon after, and that was two humans living with us. I couldn't allow them to destroy the clan."

Sebastian's mouth tasted like ash. He understood what Caven was saying and that Caven's father had pushed him in a direction he should never have taken. That didn't make it easier to accept. Caven had been an adult, and he hadn't needed to do what his father wanted him to do. He could have said no and found another way to protect the clan. "What about Cain?"

Caven's gaze flickered to his own stomach. "The clan needs allies. My father and I have been working on our contacts with the other clans for years. When Cain's old clan said they would cut all diplomatic relationships with us if we didn't give him back, I panicked, because the clans who aren't allies are enemies. We can't afford more of those, and I did what I thought was right to avoid that situation."

Once again, Caven had a perfect explanation for what he'd done. "Do you still believe in everything you've done?" Sebastian asked.

"If you're asking me if I'd do it again, the answer is no. I know now that my father pushed me in the wrong direction and that I could have helped the clan in many other ways. But I can't change what I did. I can't change the fact that even though I thought I was doing the right thing, I wasn't. I'll understand if you feel like you can't deal with it."

Sebastian didn't know what he could and couldn't deal with. What he did know was that the Caven standing next to him wasn't the Caven he'd gotten to know, and he had no idea how to deal with *that*.

CHAPTER NINE

Sebastian wasn't the same anymore. He'd been distant since he'd found out what Caven had done to be imprisoned, and Caven didn't blame him. He also wasn't surprised. He'd always expected Sebastian to put space between them and eventually leave him once he found out what was in Caven's past, and that was what had happened.

But even though Caven had expected it and understood it, even though he didn't blame Sebastian for not wanting to talk to him, it hurt. He'd gotten used to having Sebastian in his life, and he'd thought he'd have it forever for a brief moment. It had been easy to imagine the two of them raising their child together, Sebastian settling in with the clan, and everyone forgiving Caven.

He snorted and buried his face into the nest. That had been a dream, and clearly, the dream wasn't going to come true. Now, Caven had to decide what to do.

He rolled over and stared at the ceiling. He pressed a hand to his stomach, then the other, and wondered when he'd started to spend so much time in his human form.

He could pinpoint when he had. It had everything to do with Sebastian and wanting to be close to him, to talk to him. It was also easier to sneak around in a smaller form, which was what Caven had been doing since he'd come back.

But he wasn't sneaking around anymore. Instead, he was hiding in his rooms, and he had no intention of coming out anytime soon. The only times he did were at night when everyone was asleep. He left Sebastian behind and went to the kitchens to get food because he didn't want to ask the servants to help. He wasn't hungry, but he owed it to his baby to be healthy.

But he had to face the truth. Caven already loved the child growing inside of him. It was just an egg for now, but Caven already felt the need to do everything he could to ensure his child was all right.

And maybe that wasn't staying with them.

It was easy to imagine what would happen if Caven stayed with the clan and had the baby. As long as he was involved in the baby's life, people wouldn't treat the child the way they should. They wouldn't hurt them, not physically, but there were so many ways to hurt someone. It was bad enough that the baby wouldn't be able to change who his father was. At least if Caven was gone, they'd be able to live their life without his shadow hanging over them.

Caven hadn't talked to Sebastian about this yet, but he would have to soon. If he decided to leave, he could do it as soon as he laid the egg, and it wouldn't be that long before it happened. A few months, and he'd be free to go and leave his child with Sebastian.

Sebastian would be a good father. He was a good person, and he loved the baby, even though it wouldn't be easy for him to raise them on his own. But then, he wouldn't truly be on his own. He'd have the clan and possibly, his family. They'd been worried about Sebastian disappearing so quickly, but he'd called them once they'd reached the palace, and he'd explained what had happened and that he was safe. He'd always be safe with the clan, and so would their child.

A knock on the door made Caven frown. He got to his feet, something that was getting harder every day that passed with his stomach growing.

Sebastian had left earlier, telling Caven he was getting something to eat. He wouldn't knock, but who else could it be? Maybe his hands were full and he couldn't open the door on his own. Maybe he'd brought something to eat for Caven. Even though he was barely talking to Caven, he was still taking care of him in a way that made Caven want to cry.

Caven opened the door and instantly wished he hadn't.

His father stood there, glaring at him. The glare deepened when he looked down and his gaze stopped on Caven's stomach.

"So it's true," he said.

Caven's first instinct was to slam the door in his father's face, but he'd known he'd have to see him eventually. He supposed now was as good a moment as any.

He stepped aside. "Do you want to come in?" He didn't want his father to, but it would be better than having a shouting match in the middle of the hallway. As far as Caven knew, no one was aware of the fact that he hated his father and that they didn't have a good relationship.

Caven's father was controlling in every aspect of Caven's life, and Caven had always hated that. He'd never done anything to change it until he'd been imprisoned and had then escaped. His father wasn't going to like what Caven had to tell him, just like he didn't like the fact that Caven was pregnant.

Caven's father walked in. He looked around, and Caven could almost read his thoughts. But he didn't care what his father thought of the place where he lived. These rooms were his home, at least for now, and they were the place where his child would grow up.

Caven's father turned to look at him. "You're a disappointment," he said. His voice had gone cold, like always when he was angry.

Caven resisted the urge to wrap his arms around himself. His father would latch on the gesture if he did. "I'm sure you think I am," he said.

His father stepped forward. He'd never been violent, and Caven didn't expect him to start now. He would never dirty his hands with blood, although he wouldn't hesitate to ask someone else to do so. He wouldn't even care if it hurt the baby, because he didn't want Caven to be pregnant.

"What do you think you're doing? How could you allow that human to get you pregnant? That was something only your consort should have been allowed to do."

"You mean only someone you'd approved of."

"Exactly! And a human? Don't you have any respect for yourself and for our family? How do you think it looks to our allies?" He shook his head. "There's only one thing to do. You'll get rid of the egg, and you'll come home. I'll keep an eye on you until I'm sure you're back in your right mind. Then, we'll get back to work."

Furry coursed through Caven. "No," he said. He didn't think he'd ever gone against his father's orders, and it showed.

His father's eyes widened and his skin darkened. For a moment, he stared at Caven as if he couldn't quite believe what Caven had said. Caven couldn't, either. He'd never had this kind of courage.

"What did you say?" Caven's father asked.

Caven drew himself taller. "That I won't do any of what you just demanded. I won't *get rid* of the egg, and I won't go back to working with you. I'm done with all of that."

"You'll obey my orders as you've always done. It's the only way for you to survive and for the clan to thrive."

"That's not true. Ita has been doing a good job as our queen, and I'm on her side. I should never have listened to you to begin with, and I should have known that you were doing all of this for your own gain. You never cared about the clan's safety. You just cared that you wanted to be in charge, that you wanted the power to be yours, and you'd have gotten it through me. If I'd ended up on the throne, I have no doubt you would have taken control. That's over now."

Everything was over as far as Caven was concerned. He might be about to lose the only home he'd ever known, and for good this time, but before he left, he'd make sure his cousin knew what his father was planning what he'd been doing over the years. It was the least he could do.

For everyone he'd ever hurt.

When Sebastian heard the screams, he knew something was wrong. He dumped the bag in which he'd stuffed enough food for both himself and Caven and ran toward their rooms. He was sure the yelling came from there, and he was terrified of what he'd find once he reached it.

Caven wouldn't have opened the door to anyone, right? He knew better than to put himself in danger, especially with the baby.

But then, why were there two men screaming inside of the rooms?

Sebastian stumbled as he reached their door and threw it open. He rushed in to find Caven standing in front of another turquoise dragon. This dragon's color was darker, and he looked older. Sebastian was starting to recognize when a dragon was male and when they were female, and he was pretty sure this was a male, especially because of the voice.

The older dragon and Caven looked like each other.

Caven looked like this dragon who was screaming at him, and that was almost enough to make Sebastian stop. But in the end, he didn't care who the dragon was. He only cared that the asshole was screaming at Caven and that he shouldn't be allowed to.

Sebastian placed himself between Caven and the other dragon. He wouldn't stand a chance in a fight if the dragon shifted, or even only if he tried hurting him while he was in his human form, but he didn't care. He'd protect Caven and their baby, even if it meant his death.

"What do you think you're doing?" the dragon screamed.

It was intimidating. There was no way around that, and Sebastian was so scared he wouldn't have been surprised if he'd pissed his pants. But he was starting to learn how to deal with dragons, and he knew they'd never respect him if he didn't show them he was strong. So he stood up against the dragon, glaring at him.

"What do *you* think you're doing?" he snapped. "How dare you scream at Caven the way you are?"

"Do you know who I am?" the dragon asked.

"I have no idea, and I don't care. As far as I'm concerned, you're an asshole, and you need to leave."

The dragon gaped. Sebastian took the opportunity to slightly turn around so he could look at Caven, who was standing behind him. "Are you all right?"

Caven nodded. "I am. You didn't have to step in, though."

"How can you say that? This asshole was screaming at you."

The corners of Caven's lips curled. "He was, but I'm used to it."

Sebastian frowned. "What?"

"Sebastian, meet my father, Lyndon."

In any other circumstance, Sebastian would have been mortified. This wasn't how he'd imagined meeting Caven's parents.

But he knew what he'd stepped in on. He'd heard what Lyndon was saying about Caven, and it was enough for him not to want to get to know the asshole.

He crossed his arms over his chest and glared at Lyndon. "I don't care who he is. I don't want him here near you or the baby. It's clear he's an asshole, and that's all I need to know."

"I'll have your head," Lyndon threatened.

"You can try, but the queen likes me. Somehow, I doubt she'll go along with what you want."

Lyndon's gaze moved to Caven. "How can you allow him to talk to me that way? How could you allow any of this to happen? I thought you'd lost it when you were imprisoned, but that was just the tip, wasn't it? What happened to you?"

"What happened to him was that he found his conscience," Sebastian answered for Caven. "Something you clearly can't say. Caven is a better dragon than you can ever hope of being, and I won't let you hurt him like you have in the past. You know where the door is. Use it."

Sebastian should never have left Caven alone. Even more importantly, they should have talked a while ago. Sebastian should have told Caven that he couldn't stop loving him even after he'd found out about him, even after knowing what Caven had done.

It had been confusing and painful, and he still didn't fully understand how Caven could have done it. But none of that mattered. Caven wasn't the dragon he'd been when he'd been imprisoned. Something had changed, and Sebastian liked to think that it was thanks to him, too. Most of it was because of Caven, though. He could have left Sebastian to his fate and abandoned him with Patrick O'Neill. Instead, he'd stepped in and had saved him, and it had changed both their lives in a way neither of them could have expected.

But Sebastian had wanted to know more about what happened. Over the past few days, he'd talked to Morven again and with the other people in Morven's family. He knew what Caven had done to Sheldon, Blake, and Cain. He wasn't sure they'd ever be able to forgive Caven, but that was okay. They'd been hurt, and Sebastian didn't blame them for being angry or hating Caven. Caven didn't need these people to love him.

He just needed Sebastian.

And he also really fucking needed for his father to leave him alone.

Sebastian pointed at the door. "I'm waiting for you to leave. Or do you want me to call the guards? I'm sure you're aware that you're in the royal wing."

Finally, Lyndon moved. Sebastian and Caven would be long dead if his scowl could have set things on fire. As it was, scowling was the only thing Lyndon could do as he stomped toward the door.

"You're not part of our family anymore," he said, his hand on the door handle. "I don't have a son. As far as I'm concerned, you don't exist."

Sebastian's heart broke for Caven. Even though Lyndon was clearly an asshole, he was still Caven's father. He was the man who'd raised Caven—albeit poorly—and losing him couldn't be easy, even though it was for the best.

Maybe Sebastian would call his father and ask him to come. He had enough love for Sebastian to share it with Caven.

The door slammed behind Lyndon. Sebastian stared at it for a moment longer, almost afraid Lyndon would come back. Once he was sure that wouldn't happen, he turned to Caven and reached for him. "Are you all right?"

Caven nodded and to Sebastian's dismay, stepped away, not allowing him to touch him.

"It needed to be done," he said.

"I agree you had to talk to him, but I don't like that you did so on your own in our rooms. What would have happened if he'd turned violent?"

"He wouldn't get his hands dirty. The only thing he could do was disown me, and you heard him. I don't exist anymore."

"Well, that's his problem. It means he'll lose out on

meeting his grandchild."

Caven nodded, but his expression was blank. Something was wrong, and while Sebastian wanted to put it all on Lyndon's shoulders, he couldn't. He'd been distant, and he'd hurt Caven. Instead of not talking to him, he should have explained that he needed some time and space. But he'd shut Caven out, and clearly, Caven expected him to do so again.

"I've been thinking," Caven said.

"So have I."

Caven nodded and swallowed. "I realize that you can't forgive me for what I've done in the past. I never expected you to, but I'm grateful for our time together. I also know that as long as I'm here, the clan won't treat you and our child the way they should. If you're willing to do so, you should raise the baby on your own. I'll leave as soon as I lay the egg, and it will be like I never existed, just like my father said."

Sebastian was going to strangle Lyndon if he ever managed to get his hands on him.

"No," he said.

Caven frowned. "What do you mean?"

"Exactly what I said. No, I'm not willing to raise the child on my own. I'm not willing to let you leave. We're a family, you, me, and the baby. None of us is going anywhere."

"But after what happened—"

"I don't care about what happened. I don't care what you did. You're a different person now, and I truly believe that. Besides, I love you. How could I let you leave?"

"You love me?"

It was time to close the distance Sebastian had put between them. He'd been an idiot, and he vowed never to do something so stupid again. He'd hurt Caven, which was the last thing he ever wanted to do.

He moved forward and wrapped his arms around Caven's waist. He could feel the slight bump there, and while he was in awe like always when he thought of the baby, he was also angry at himself for what he'd almost lost.

"I love you and the baby," he said. "That's never going to change. You can leave if it's what you want, but I really hope you'll stay."

Caven's arms wrapped around Sebastian. "As long as it's what you want, I will," Caven whispered.

"Stay."

CHAPTER TEN

Caven had been wary of answering any knocks on the door since his father had visited. Sebastian felt the same, which was why they'd stuck together. Since they'd talked and had smoothed things out between them, Caven felt more secure, about both his place next to Sebastian and his place with the clan. Sebastian had become Caven's protector, which wasn't something either of them had expected after the way they'd met. Caven didn't mind, though. He quite enjoyed being able to rely on Sebastian.

"I'll open the door," Sebastian said.

Caven was in their nest, resting. Every time he tried getting up, Sebastian glared at him and asked him what he was doing. So he stayed where he was and watched as Sebastian went to the door.

Sebastian tensed at the sight of whoever was there, so Caven sat up. Sebastian had made friends with several dragons, including the people Caven had been an asshole to—which, to be honest, was almost everyone in the clan. He was even friends with Sheldon and Blake, although that possibly had more to do with the fact that they were the only three humans in the clan. But whoever was at the door, Sebastian didn't like it, and Caven was ready to step in if he had to.

"Slavin, Octavia," Sebastian said.

Caven swallowed. He reminded himself that his cousin had told him she'd want to talk to him eventually and that she wasn't putting him back in his cell. She was a dragon of her word, and if she'd said he was free, then he was free.

"The queen wants to see Caven," Slavin explained.

Sebastian turned to Caven, who was already getting to his feet. He rushed to Caven to help him, even though Caven didn't need it yet. His stomach was growing bigger every day, but it would be several weeks before Caven was ready to lay the egg. He wasn't going to stay in the nest the entire time, no matter what Sebastian was trying to convince him of.

"We can go," Caven said.

"But I'm coming with you," Sebastian said, his tone uncompromising. He took Caven's hand and stared at Slavin and Octavia as if daring them to say something about it.

Slavin grinned. "The queen said she expected you to be there, too."

"Good, because he's not going anywhere without me."

Octavia was still staring at Caven, and he steeled himself for whatever she had to say. He'd never done anything to her personally, but he'd tried hurting her friends, the mates of the people she loved the most. He wouldn't be surprised if she held a grudge against him.

Instead, she smiled. "Hello," she said. "How are you feeling? Are you sure you're up to walking to the throne room?"

"I'm perfectly fine," Caven told her. "Even though Sebastian seems to think that I'll break down if I as much as brush my teeth."

Octavia laughed as they all moved into the hallway. "My sister was very much the same when her mate was pregnant," she said. "It's been years, but I still remember how much they fought over it."

"Sebastian and I haven't been fighting."

"That's good. How are you feeling? I've never been pregnant, but I can imagine it's not easy."

"It was unexpected, but both Sebastian and I are over the moon happy about it."

"I never expected you to date a human," Slavin blurted out.

He seemed unrepentant. "I mean, considering the way you behaved before, I'd never have thought you'd even talk to a human without sounding disgusted."

And there was Caven's past coming back to bite him in the ass again. "You're not wrong. If all of this had happened a year ago, well, it wouldn't have happened. When I found Sebastian being threatened, I wouldn't have stepped in to save him."

"So you really changed. Morven told me about it, but I wasn't sure I believed him."

"He changed before we met," Sebastian piped in. "You just heard him. He wouldn't have saved me if he hadn't already been changing. People seem to think that he is the way he is now only because of me, but that's not true. Caven has never been a bad person. He just did bad things, and he's sorry he did them. It's a bit the clan's fault, though."

Sebastian had been ranting about this since he'd met Caven's father, but Caven wished he wasn't making his opinion public.

"What do you mean?" Octavia asked. Thankfully, she didn't look angry but rather puzzled.

"Have you met Caven's father? Because he's an asshole. The other day I found him screaming at Caven, and he said Caven wasn't his son anymore and that as far as he was concerned, Caven doesn't exist. That's abusive behavior. If someone had noticed how abusive Lyndon was and had done something about it, like maybe removing Caven, Caven would never have done what he did."

Caven was relieved when they reached the throne room. It was close to the royal wing, which gave Sebastian less time to talk. He took Sebastian's hand and dragged him inside, nodding at the guards standing by the doors. Octavia and Slavin didn't follow them, but they didn't need to. Ita wasn't alone. Morven and Orran were with her, the three of them talking.

They looked up, and Ita smiled. "There you are. I have something to ask you, and while I know it's a lot, I hope you'll say yes."

"I can tell you everything," Caven said.

To his surprise, she shook her head. "I'm certainly curious to hear all of it, but that's not why I wanted to see you. Do you need to sit?"

"I just need to hear what you have to say. You're making me nervous."

"That wasn't my intention, so I'll go straight to the point. I'd like for you to work with me. You know how the meetings with the other clans went, so you're aware of the fact that while some of the clans agree with us and our stand when it comes to humans, not all of them do. I'd like you to contact the others and try to work on an alliance between clans. I realize we're never all going to think the same, but in some circumstances, it's important we agree."

"I can certainly talk to some of the leaders, but I can't make promises when it comes to convincing them to be on our side," Caven warned her.

This wasn't what he'd expected. He was pretty sure no one had, not even Ita's closest advisors. If Caven hadn't behaved the way he had, it would have been normal for her to ask him to do this, since they were cousins. They'd grown up together and had been taught by the same teachers. As it was, most of the clan dragons still wondered why Caven wasn't locked up. For the queen to give him such an important role was something many dragons would have a problem with.

Caven didn't care

"I realize that," Ita said. "And I don't expect you to work miracles. But not all clans were present at the meetings, and I'm sure we can convince some of those who were to change their mind. I also want you and Sebastian to be present when I meet the human delegation. It will be good for them to see that the humans who live with us are perfectly fine and happy. I'd also like your input on them and to know what you think of them. I have little experience with humans, so I'm not sure what to expect."

"We'll be happy to help," Caven said.

"As long as Caven can get enough rest and is careful," Sebastian agreed.

Caven wasn't surprised, but he needed to do this. He'd never be able to undo the pain he'd caused, but he'd do whatever he could in order to fix things. That meant keeping the clan safe—the right way this time, by helping Ita.

"We'll be there," he confirmed.

After walking Caven back to their rooms, Sebastian went in search of food. Caven had said he didn't need anything, but Sebastian had developed a protective streak a mile long, at least when it came to Caven. Maybe it was because Caven had saved him, or because he was pregnant. Sebastian didn't know, and he honestly didn't care. He just wanted to take care of Caven, and Caven was letting him, for some reason.

Caven was a dragon shifter. He didn't need Sebastian to protect him from anything, and he certainly didn't need him to bring him food. Yet when Sebastian had told him he was going to the dining hall, he'd smiled and said he'd be waiting in their rooms.

Sebastian had noticed Caven had been doing that a lot. It was understandable, but Sebastian didn't like it. He wanted Caven to be able to live his life, make friends, be with others. He understood why most of the clan was wary of him, but couldn't they see he'd changed?

Sebastian snorted softly. How could they see he'd changed when he was hiding? Sebastian wanted to help, but he wasn't sure there was anything he could do in this situation. It was something Caven would have to do by himself.

When Sebastian reached the dining hall, he made a beeline for the tables where the food was displayed. He grabbed a tray and two plates and started filling them, but the sound of someone laughing made him turn.

He couldn't stop looking at the humans. They looked odd sitting in the middle of dragon shifters, but then Sebastian supposed he did, too. He'd talked to them a few times, just like he'd talked to Cain, but he didn't feel he was part of their group. How could he be, when he was with Caven?

He didn't blame any of them for not wanting to be his friend. They weren't in school anymore, and if they wanted nothing to do with him, then he was fine with it. But he didn't want people to dislike him, especially for something like being in love.

This time, there was one more reason for Sebastian to stare at the group of friends. They weren't alone. Three baby dragons were with them, and once Sebastian noticed them, he *really* started staring.

He knew who the babies were. He recognized the blue one as the queen's son, while the green one was Morven and Sheldon's daughter. She kept shifting back and forth between her human and her dragon forms, and when she was in her dragon form, she stole food from plates. Sheldon was trying to get her to stop, but she didn't seem to want to. Every time he scolded her, she gave him a toothless human smile, then shifted back to her dragon form.

The last baby was dark yellow. Sebastian knew the story, so he knew that Hogan wasn't Lorne's father. He still looked like he could be and like Lorne was the perfect mix of Hogan and Cain.

By the time Sebastian was done watching the babies, someone at the table had noticed him. Sheldon was staring at him as hard as he was staring at Sheldon and the babies, and

Sebastian looked away, his cheeks flushing. He hadn't meant for anyone to realize what he was doing, although he supposed he hadn't exactly been discreet. That would teach him. He needed to keep his distance until people managed to forget what Caven had done.

Sebastian suspected it would take a while.

He grabbed the tray he'd filled with food and moved toward the door, but a movement next to him made him stop before he could. Sheldon stood there, smiling at him, and it was enough to make Sebastian turn around to make sure there wasn't someone behind him. It didn't make sense that Sheldon was smiling. He'd talked to Sebastian before, but that was because they wanted Sebastian to know about Caven. Since he had no intention of leaving Caven, surely they wouldn't want anything to do with him.

Right?

"You're watching the babies," Sheldon said.

It made more sense now. He was angry because Sebastian had been staring. "I'm sorry. It's just that I didn't know dragons could turn into humans until a few months ago, and now, I'm about to have a child who can go back and forth between human and dragon. It feels unreal, and I guess watching the babies helps. I won't do it again."

Sheldon shook his head. "That's not why I'm here." He hesitated and looked back at the table. "Although I can understand why you think it is. We haven't treated you right, have we?"

Sebastian swallowed. "You've treated me the only way you wanted to treat me. I understand you don't want to be my friend or even that you don't want anything to do with me. Considering the fact that I'm with Caven and what he did to you, I don't blame you."

"But you had nothing to do with what happened."

"Maybe not, but some people will see me being with Caven as me approving of what he did."

"And you don't?"

Sebastian glared. "Of course not. Caven himself disapproves of what he did, but no one knows that because no one wants to talk to him. None of you has any idea what he went through. You only see what he wants to show you and what his father allowed him to show. No one ever wondered why he was doing what he did. No one ever wondered if there was something more behind it."

Sebastian snapped his mouth shut. Caven had already told him not to mention his father to anyone and not scold the clan for not seeing that his father was abusing him. Sebastian wasn't sure how he felt about that, but he'd promised and wanted to keep his promises.

Sheldon frowned. "You're serious."

"I wouldn't be saying it if I weren't. Look, I understand why you hate him. He did terrible things. But you don't know *why* he did those things, just like you don't know how much he's changed. He didn't want to do any of that, but no one would have helped him if he'd said anything. He wouldn't have allowed those other dragons to take Cain, you know? He was only trying to keep everyone happy, including people he shouldn't have been keeping happy. But none of you realized that. You never tried to get to know him, and you haven't given him the benefit of the doubt. I don't blame you for it, but I wish you could at least stop hating him long enough to see that he's been trying to fix things."

Sheldon stared for a moment longer. Sebastian had no idea what the man was thinking, and honestly, he didn't care. He needed to get back to Caven, so he tightened his hold on the tray and moved toward the door.

But Sheldon wasn't done with him. He grabbed Sebastian's wrist to stop him.

Sebastian stopped, his heart racing. He had no idea what was about to happen, but he hoped it wouldn't be bad. He might have Caven, but he needed friends. He needed the clan to accept him, and he wasn't sure if that would ever happen.

"I just wanted to tell you that if you have any questions or want to talk, you can come to me," Sheldon said.

"What do you mean?"

"As far as I know, Morven and I are the only ones who have a human-dragon hybrid daughter. We went through a lot while Morven was pregnant and while we waited for the egg to hatch. Before she was born, there was no way for us to know what would happen and whether the baby would be healthy, and it was terrifying. Now we know that dragons and humans can have children together, so I suppose you don't have to be worried about that, but there are plenty of other things to be worried about, and I remember them well. If you ever need anything, to talk or something more practical, just come to me."

Sebastian wasn't sure how to take that. "What about Caven? Can he come to you, too? Because *he's* having this baby."

Sheldon looked at the table where his friends were sitting. Sebastian expected him to say no, but instead, to his surprise, Sheldon nodded. "I think you're right," he said. "I think we were too quick to judge Caven and what he did without asking questions. I guess we all thought that he was doing it because he wanted power and to be king. It was hard to see anything else back then, but I believe you if you say there's more. I've been watching him, although it hasn't been easy since he stays in your rooms most of the time. He acts differently, and Morven has assured me that's the case. I wasn't sure whether or not to believe him, but even if I don't, maybe I can give Caven a chance."

That was all Sebastian wanted. "Thank you."

"I'm not making promises," Sheldon warned. "But we'll try."

"It's more than enough." And hopefully, once they saw that Caven didn't mean anyone harm, they could become friends.

Sebastian missed his family. He didn't miss anything else of his old life, but his family had been the center of his life, and now he didn't have them. Phone calls and video calls were good, but it wasn't the same. The problem was that he couldn't go to them. He was terrified that somehow he'd lead Patrick O'Neill to them and that he'd hurt them to get to him. Hopefully, having friends here would help fill the hole their absence had left in Sebastian's life and his heart.

And Sebastian and Caven would *need* friends once the baby was born. Sebastian had no idea what to do with a newborn, especially one who could turn into a dragon.

CHAPTER ELEVEN

Caven wanted to rage, throw something at the wall, and possibly shift and burn the computer to the ground. Instead, he plastered a smile on his face and stared at the dragon on the screen. "You have to see that this wouldn't be good for your clan," he told Bergen.

"What wouldn't be good is for me to align my clan with our enemies."

Caven gritted his teeth. "The Ogorth clan isn't your enemy."

"They've always been our enemies."

"We're not talking about the past here. We're talking about the future and the fact that humans are trying to find a way to make this work. It won't work if some dragon clans decide to do whatever they want." Like attacking innocent humans, which Caven had no doubt Bergen had thought about.

"And you think I care? Let the humans come. My clan will show them what happens to puny humans who try to take on dragons."

Caven had always despised Bergen. The dragon was a close friend of Caven's father, which was enough for Caven not to want anything to do with him. He'd even wondered if Bergen and his father somehow had something to do with how the humans had found them during the meetings. Someone had to have told them where the meetings were being held. There would have been no other way for them to get there, catch so many dragons unprepared, and hurt them.

But Caven had no proof. He had nothing more than

suspicions, and they weren't enough. As it was, he and the Ogorth clan needed to make alliances with the other clans. The meetings had failed, and Caven was, too.

At least with Bergen. Some other clans had agreed to ally with the Ogorth clan regarding the humans. It was better than nothing, and it was something Caven wanted to take advantage of in other ways, but right now, he needed to focus on what the humans would think if Bergen and his clan decided to do something stupid.

Hopefully, they'd understand that not all clans were the same and wouldn't blame the Ogorth clan for whatever Bergen was about to do.

Caven had known he wouldn't be able to convince Bergen. He'd had to try, but he wasn't surprised about any of this. He'd warned the queen it wouldn't work, and she'd told him she didn't expect it to, even though she wanted him to try. Well, he had, and now, he was done with Bergen.

"Your father contacted me," Bergen said.

Caven stiffened. The smile he was faking slipped a bit, but he thought he managed to get it back into place before Bergen noticed. "The two of you are old friends," he said.

"We are. I can't tell you how disappointed I was to hear what you're doing with your life. A human, Caven?"

"Sebastian is worth your entire clan," Caven spat out. "Don't you dare mention him ever again. He's the gentlest human being, and I won't allow anyone to hurt him, including you and my father."

Bergen seemed amused. Caven knew he shouldn't lose control like this, especially not with these people, but he couldn't stop himself. When his father had sneered at Sebastian, Caven had wanted to strangle him. He wanted to do the same with Bergen, which would be harder, considering he was thousands of miles away. The only thing Caven could do was glare at his image on the screen.

"I suppose I'm not surprised," Bergen said. "I always wondered if you'd be up to the task, and I suspected you weren't. I told your father that he needed to be the one to take Ita's place, although I suppose that's a moot point now. I was surprised to see that she hasn't had him arrested yet."

That was because she didn't have any proof of what Caven's father had been doing beyond Caven's word. Caven wanted to give her much more, but his father wasn't stupid. He'd made sure there would be no proof of his involvement or of what he and Caven had done.

Since he wasn't going to convince Bergen of anything, Caven hung up without saying goodbye. It was satisfying to press the button and see Bergen's image disappear, although he wished he could have reached through the screen and shaken the dragon a little first.

Bergen and Caven's father were alike, which probably explained why they'd become friends and allies.

Caven sighed and flopped back into his chair. He rubbed his forehead, hoping the headache threatening to bloom would vanish rather than stick around. He had work to do, and he wouldn't be able to do it if Sebastian realized he had a headache.

Sebastian had gone into overprotective mode, and while Caven was amused, he couldn't say he hated it. He couldn't remember the last time someone had taken care of him the way Sebastian was. Caven realized it had a lot to do with the baby and with the fact that Sebastian cared about him. He wanted Caven to be happy and healthy, and he was making sure he had everything he needed to make the laying of the egg as easy as possible.

Caven wouldn't have expected this from a human before, but Sheldon was one of the most affectionate and loving fathers he'd ever seen, and he wasn't a dragon. Children weren't as precious to humans as they were to dragons, yet to

Sheldon, his daughter was the center of the world.

Caven had always known there was more to humans than what his father wanted him to see, but he hadn't been able to find out what that was until he'd met some of them. Now he knew, and he couldn't help but wonder if Blake and Sheldon would eventually forgive him. He didn't need them to become his friends, although he couldn't say he would mind. No, he mostly wanted Sebastian to have people like him to talk to. It couldn't be easy for him to be away from his family and the place he'd called home all his life. Everything around Sebastian had changed, and Caven was a big reason for that.

The asshole who'd tried to kill him was another.

Caven opened his eyes and stared at the screen. He had a list of clan leaders who'd agreed to be on the Ogorth clan's side when it came to humans, and some were even sending representatives to the meeting with the humans. Caven wasn't looking forward to that meeting, but it had to be done. The queen herself had asked him to be present, and he suspected it was because she wanted to show the clan that she trusted him. He still didn't understand how she could and why she did, but he was done asking.

His cousin wasn't like his father. She wasn't plotting anything against Caven. If she wanted him to be there, she no doubt believed that his presence would be beneficial to the clan. So Caven would go.

"You're still working?" Sebastian asked from the door of the room Caven had turned into an office. They also had a spare nest room for the baby when they came, and their own room and a sitting area.

Caven was already smiling as he turned to look at him. He couldn't help it. Everything Sebastian said or did made him smile. "I am."

"You should get some rest. Working so much isn't good for you or the baby."

"Maybe not, but there's plenty of things to do before the meetings."

"I realize that. I'm not saying you have to stop working. Just slow down, especially when you talk to assholes like that guy."

Caven wasn't surprised Sebastian had heard the conversation with Bergen. "It had to be done, but now that I know he won't have anything to do with this, I can stop pandering to him."

"Good. Now come to bed."

Caven did. After he was done working, it was good to be able to forget about everything and focus on Sebastian. Caven had never had anything like this, and he never wanted to lose it.

He settled in their nest on his back, and Sebastian cuddled against him. They were silent for a moment, the only sounds their breathing.

Then Sebastian wiggled until he could look up at Caven. "I saw the babies today," he said.

Caven didn't have to ask which babies he was talking about. "In the dining hall?"

"Yeah. I also talked to Sheldon. He said that if I ever need any advice on dealing with our baby, I could go to him."

"Well, he knows what you're about to go through with our baby."

"He's the only one who does."

"Are the two of you friends?" Caven wanted the answer to be yes, but he wouldn't be surprised if it was no.

Sebastian didn't deserve to be hated and kept at a distance, but he was with Caven, which was enough for most of the people in the clan not to want anything to do with him. Sometimes, Caven wondered if he should break up with him. Then he remembered how stubborn Sebastian was, and he knew that even if he tried, Sebastian wouldn't allow him to.

"I suppose we're friendly," Sebastian said. "We talked a few times, and I hope it'll lead to more. I want friends."

Caven kissed Sebastian's forehead. "And you should have them. You should have everything you've ever wanted." And if that everything was something Caven could give him, then Caven would.

Sebastian wanted everyone to get along and be happy, even though it was unreasonable. He wasn't sure it would ever happen, but he hoped that his tentative new friends would at least tolerate Caven's presence.

Sebastian wanted friends, but he wanted Caven to have friends, too. He'd been isolating himself, and while he acted as if it didn't matter, it did. He shouldn't have to be on his own, alone in their rooms. He shouldn't have to hide because most of the clan hated him. He'd done what he'd done, but he regretted it and had apologized. He'd spent time in jail. Why was he still paying for all of that?

Sebastian realized that he probably thought that way because he was in love with Caven. Most other people wouldn't want anything to do with him, as was the case with the clan. But Sebastian loved Caven, and he wanted him to be happy.

"You could come to lunch with me tomorrow," he suggested.

Sebastian waited, knowing Caven didn't want to expose himself that way. Still, eventually, he'd need to come out of their rooms, if not for himself, for their baby. When the baby was born, they'd need a family, people who would care about them. They wouldn't get that if Caven hid away the entire time. There was no better moment for him to make friends than right now, and Sebastian wanted him to see that.

"You understand why I haven't been coming with you, right?" Caven asked.

"I do, and I won't force you to do anything. But I believe that one of the reasons people still don't trust you is because you haven't shown them who you are. Most of them don't know what you're doing with the queen or that you're helping the clan and fixing your relationship with her. Besides, I think Sheldon and the others want to talk to you."

"I doubt they do. You know what I did to them."

Sebastian propped himself up on his elbow so he could look down at Caven. "I know what you did, just like I know how much you regret it and that your father pushed you to do things you aren't proud of."

"My father might have pushed me, but I'm an adult. I should have said no, and I should have told my cousin what my father was doing. Instead, I went along with what he wanted. I hurt Sheldon and Blake, and I kidnapped Cain. How can they ever forgive me for what I did?"

It broke Sebastian's heart to hear Caven sounding so hopeless. "I'm not promising they will. But Sheldon and Blake seem to be fine with me. Cain is the one I have the hardest time talking to. It's as if he expects me to hurt him just because I'm with you."

Caven stroked Sebastian's arm. "I'm sorry. I know how important it is to you to make friends."

"It is, but I understand why Cain feels that way. I think it would be good for him to see that you won't hurt him. I'm not saying all of this will be easy, but we won't know if we can fix anything if we don't try."

"This is important to you."

That was an understatement, but Sebastian nodded anyway.

He wanted Caven to become a true part of the clan. He wanted him to see that no matter what his father had pushed him to do, he hadn't ruined his chances of having a clan. Caven could work with his cousin, keep the clan safe, and make friends. He could create a family that his father would have no hope of influencing.

He could be happy, no matter what he kept telling himself.

Sebastian might not be able to read Caven's mind, but he could tell when Caven started thinking badly of himself. He wanted that to stop, and while it would take time, he felt that making friends with the people he'd tried to hurt would help. Of course, if they wanted nothing to do with Caven, they'd have to find another way. Sebastian wouldn't blame them.

But he hoped they'd give him a chance, just like they'd given him one. No matter what had happened, Caven wasn't a bad person.

"I wish I could take you to your family," Caven murmured.

"I don't want to go back. My place is here now, with you and our baby."

Sebastian pressed a hand to Caven's stomach. It was big now, heavy, and from what Caven had said, it wouldn't be long before he was ready to lay the egg. Unfortunately, that didn't mean they'd meet their baby right away. Dragons didn't work like humans, and while Sebastian was impatient, he just wanted his child to be healthy. It didn't matter when they were born, although he hoped he'd be able to have his family with him when it happened.

"But you want to see them," Caven said.

"Of course I do. They still have a hard time believing that you and I are having a child. I want them to be here when it happens, but I'm terrified that Patrick will hurt them. What if he somehow finds out I visited them? For now, they're safe, but as soon as I step back in their life, they could get hurt, and I don't want that to happen."

Caven hummed as he thought. "Maybe we could get rid of Patrick," he said hesitantly. "I understand that you don't want anyone to die, but you'll be able to do whatever you want with him gone."

"I won't deny that it's tempting to say yes." Sebastian had thought about it. How could he not? But he wasn't a killer, and he wasn't about to send Caven to kill Patrick, especially in his state. "But I don't want to be like him. Maybe we could just threaten him?"

"What do you mean?"

"Well, what if I landed on his doorstep with a team of dragons? He won't be afraid of me, and he might even not be afraid of one or two dragons, but how about an entire group of them? What if they threaten to eat him if he does anything?" Sebastian sat up. He was excited by his idea, even though he didn't know if it could work. "We can even force him to go to the police and confess what he did to that woman. Then he'll be behind bars, and I wouldn't have to worry about him ever again." He turned to look at Caven. "What do you think?"

Caven looked thoughtful. "Well, we can certainly mention this to Ita. She likes you, and she's asked me if I thought that moving your family to the palace would make you happy."

Sebastian gaped. "What did you tell her?"

"That I'd ask you. And yes, I know it would. I also know it might not be as easy as we wish. They have lives, jobs, and homes. They might not be willing to drop everything to move in with a bunch of dragons. If they can't, we'll have to keep them safe in a different way, and making sure the man who tried to kill you is behind bars would certainly take care of that. I don't think my cousin will say no to this plan, but considering how close we are to the meeting with the humans, we need to be careful."

Sebastian nodded. He didn't care what happened to Patrick, but he understood where Caven was coming from. Caven had to think of the entire clan, not just of Sebastian.

But it felt good to have something to offer his family. The next time he called them, Sebastian would tell them that the queen had suggested they move to the palace. He'd tell them that they had a plan to deal with Patrick O'Neill and that even if they couldn't come, they'd be safe.

Things were looking up. Sebastian was making friends, and Caven had agreed to come to lunch with him tomorrow. Sebastian's family might be about to move into the palace with the dragons.

What more could Sebastian want from life?

He squeaked when Caven rolled them until Sebastian was under him. Caven's cock slid out of his pouch, and Sebastian grinned.

This. This was the more he could want — and the more he'd get.

CHAPTER TWELVE

Caven could never say no to Sebastian, which was the only reason he was headed toward the dining hall to have lunch. Sebastian was bouncing next to him, clearly happy, which was why Caven was on board with doing this. Caven would have stayed in his rooms if Sebastian had been anyone else. As it was, he was so nervous he doubted he'd be able to eat.

That wouldn't stop him from trying.

He wanted Sebastian to be happy, and apparently this was part of it. Caven hoped the others would behave, because he didn't know how he'd react if they hurt Sebastian. He needed to keep in mind that Sebastian wouldn't like it if he was growly, but he had no idea what was about to happen, and it was hard to view their lunch as something good.

Sebastian grabbed Caven's hand and linked their fingers together. "You shouldn't be so nervous."

"How can I not be? You know everyone always stares when they see me. It's gotten even worse now that my stomach is so big." Caven pressed a hand against it, reassuring himself that his baby was fine.

The healers had seen him that morning, and they'd said everything was proceeding the way it should. It would be time for Caven to lay his egg in just a few weeks.

But first, they had to go through the meeting with the humans. Sebastian had made it known that he wasn't happy about the fact that Caven would have to expose himself like that while being heavily pregnant, but there was no way out of it. The queen wanted Caven there, so he'd be there. Besides, it wasn't like he was going on his own. There would be plenty of guards, and Sebastian was coming along. He was just being overprotective, but Caven didn't blame him for that. He felt very much the same way when it came to Sebastian.

From the noise, he could tell the dining hall was full. It was almost enough to make him turn around, but Sebastian squeezed his hand. That reminded Caven of why he was doing this and who he was doing it for, and he forged ahead. If the people having lunch didn't want him there, he didn't care. The only person who mattered was Sebastian.

They stepped into the hall. Just like Caven had expected, the room was full. Most dragons were in their human form because it meant more of them could fit in the room — and it was easier to eat the delicious dishes spread out on the buffet tables — but there were a few in their dragon form by the window.

Caven and Sebastian headed to get food, and Caven's stomach growled loud enough that the person standing behind him in the line chuckled. Caven narrowed his eyes and turned to look at them, the glare vanishing when he saw Blake.

He had no idea what to tell the human. He was here to show Blake and the others that he wasn't a bad person, but could he do that by keeping his mouth shut? Sebastian was the chatty one. Caven didn't talk much on the best of days, let alone when he was so nervous.

"Hungry?" Blake asked.

"Very much so," Caven answered.

"Must be the pregnancy."

"The healers did mention I have to eat a little more."

"It's good you're here, then. I haven't seen you much lately, and I was starting to wonder if you'd left again."

"No. I've just been keeping to my rooms."

Blake grimaced. "I guess it's easier for you. We haven't been very nice to you."

"I didn't expect you to be nice. I don't deserve for you to be."

To Caven's surprise, Blake waved his words away. "We should have been. I mean, I'm still angry at what you put my brother and me through, and that's without mentioning Cain, but both Morven and Orran have been telling us that you've changed. We didn't give you the opportunity to show us, which I think was wrong. Besides, if someone like Sebastian loves you, it means you're not a bad person, right?"

"I don't know about that," Caven murmured. "I'm lucky that Sebastian chose me." And he remembered that every minute of every day they spent together.

It would have been so easy for something to go wrong and for them not to have met. What if Caven had been looking for food when Sebastian was attacked? What if he'd decided not to step in, and Sebastian had died?

The thought was enough to make the anger vanish, but he still forced himself to grab food, because otherwise Sebastian would do it for him, and that never ended well. He didn't want them to fight.

"Why don't the two of you come to sit with us?" Blake suggested once he had a plate, too.

He'd chosen the pasta salad, which appeared delicious now that Caven took a better look at it. His tray was already heavy with a plate of risotto and one of salmon with vegetables, but it was tempting.

"I'll grab you a plate of pasta," Sebastian said. He sounded amused. "And thank you, Blake. We'll be happy to eat with you."

"As long as it doesn't bother anyone," Caven added.

"It won't. I made sure to ask before I came up to grab more food."

Caven wanted to stay back with Sebastian, but instead, he followed Blake through the hall. He didn't miss the way most of the dragons were staring at him, and he kept his chin high, trying to show them he didn't care what they thought. It was easier to do that when he was walking with Blake than when he was alone, or even with Sebastian.

There were two empty seats between Sheldon and Blake, right in front of Cain. The babies were here today, too, and Caven's gaze naturally strayed to them. He could hardly believe he'd have a child like that in a few months' time. He'd never expected it to happen to him, not like this. He'd always been told that he'd have to have children once he was king, but that he wouldn't be the one carrying them. His consort would, and of course, the dragon would have been someone his father had chosen.

This was so much better.

Caven sat next to Sheldon, and when Sebastian arrived, he slid into the seat between Caven and Blake. Across the table, Cain was in front of Caven, while Morven was next to him. Morven smiled at Caven when he noticed him looking, but he quickly turned his attention to his daughter in his lap.

On Cain's other side was Slavin, and next to him, his mate, Dagan. Orran and Octavia were nowhere to be seen, but it wasn't unusual to see the group missing parts. It wasn't easy to have everyone there for lunch with so many of them.

Cain stared at Caven with narrow eyes. Caven did his best not to look at him, trying not to make him angrier or freak him out. Cain's son, Lorne, was in Cain's lap, happily eating fruit from a plate on the table. He looked up at Caven and grinned, exposing his fangs. Then he snapped his head forward and snatched a square of melon.

The baby was adorable, and Caven's chest squeezed at the thought that soon he'd have one of his own.

Sheldon cleared his throat. "How are you doing? I

remember that the last weeks of the pregnancy were the hardest on Morven."

Caven forced himself to look away from Lorne. "It isn't easy to deal with how much change there is in my body, but Sebastian makes sure I get enough food and rest."

Sebastian chuckled. "If it weren't for me, he'd spend his entire days on video calls with clan leaders. I don't understand why someone else can't take care of it, especially with the asshole ones. You should have heard how one of them talked to him yesterday."

"You've been talking to other clan leaders?" Cain asked.

Caven swallowed. "I have. I'm working on an alliance between as many clans as we can convince."

"The one that should have been created during the meetings."

"Yes. Unfortunately, with the meetings ending as abruptly as they did, the clans weren't finished talking. I've been contacting the leaders to find out who's on our side and who will never be."

"And the queen trusts you to do that?"

"Apparently." Caven still didn't fully understand it, but he'd come to accept it.

Cain stared at Caven for what felt like an eternity before he finally nodded. "That's good. I can imagine it's not easy, considering your pregnancy. Have you seen the healers yet? Because it looks like you're about to lay the egg."

Caven's eyes burned. Cain hadn't said anything about what Caven had done to him, but his words spoke of acceptance, which was all Caven had wanted.

And just maybe, he'd received it.

It was good to hear Caven talk with someone about the pregnancy. Sebastian had tried to be there for him as much as possible, but he couldn't begin to comprehend what it meant for a dragon shifter to be pregnant. On the other hand, Cain had a young child, so he'd been through it recently. He and Morven were the perfect people for Caven to talk to and hopefully become friends with.

"So, tell me about your family," Sheldon said. "We've all heard the rumors, but we don't actually know much about you."

"I bet you know why I'm here, though."

"You're on the run." Sheldon leaned closer. "Don't worry. You're not the first it happened to."

Sebastian stared. "I'm not?"

Sheldon laughed. "No. I take it that no one told you how my brother and I came to be part of the clan?"

"I didn't ask, and no one volunteered that information." Sebastian had been curious, but he didn't want to be nosy.

"Well, my brother worked for some rather unappealing people. One night he found a dragon egg in his boss's office. He knew what his boss would do with the egg if he left it there, so he grabbed it and ran away."

As far as Sebastian knew, there were only a handful of baby dragons with the clan at the moment. "Blue?" he asked, certain the egg had belonged to the queen. It was the only thing that made sense.

Sheldon nodded and speared a cherry tomato with his fork. "Exactly. Blake decided he'd save the egg, even though he had no idea what to do with it. And of course, that's when Orran and his team found him. They were looking for the egg, and they demanded it back. Only Blake didn't know them, and he didn't trust them, so he decided to appoint himself temporary guardian. He and Orran ended up on the run together. It's when they fell in love, and by the time they reached the clan, they were a couple."

Sebastian was fascinated by this story. "And you?"

"Well, let's just say that my brother has never been the best at letting me know he's okay. I was worried about him, and I went looking for him. His boss decided to use me to convince Blake to bring back the egg. The clan saved me, and I've been with them since then."

"What about your family?"

Sheldon shrugged. "We weren't close. My parents thought Blake would never amount to anything because he didn't go to college and worked as a bartender. They expected too much from me, and it was a relief to be away from them." Sheldon looked at Sebastian. "I hope your family is different."

"My family is great." Sebastian was a bit sad when he thought about them, but they weren't dead. He'd see them again one day, hopefully soon. "Well, most of them. My aunt and uncle kicked my cousin out when he came out as gay, so I'd rather not see them, but Christian came to live with my family and me."

"Do you have siblings?"

"A sister, Jayna. Then there's my father, William, and my grandfather, Hyde. The three of them live together, while Christian and I have an apartment. Well, we had an apartment. I sent him home when Patrick came after me."

"I'm sure they miss you."

"And I miss them. But it's safer this way. Honestly, I'm surprised Patrick hasn't found out about them. He managed to find out where I lived, after all."

"It sounds like we need to do something about that man."

"That would be great. That way I wouldn't be terrified he'll hurt my family. Caven and I already talked to the queen, and she agreed to send a team to threaten Patrick if he doesn't leave my family and me alone. Maybe they could scare him so badly that he'll want to give himself up to the cops."

"Well, having an entire group of dragons threatening him would certainly scare him, but maybe there's something more we can do. Are you okay talking about what you saw?"

"Mostly." Sebastian still had nightmares, but it helped to know he was safe and protected.

"How about after lunch, you come to the security room and we talk about it? I can look into it, and that way, we'll know what the team will walk in on. Maybe we can even mention him to the humans we're meeting. I mean they're part of the government, right? If they know someone killed a woman, they'll have to do something about it."

Sebastian wasn't too sure about that, but he didn't want to offend Sheldon. "I suppose."

"And if they won't, we can tip off the cops. We'll make sure they have all the information you can give them."

"As long as he doesn't threaten my family, I'll be fine with anything."

Sheldon nodded. "What about your family? Are they staying back in the city? Since you seem so close to them, I thought they might come when the baby is born."

"They want to."

Sheldon got to his feet. "Then let's go. Have you asked the queen about it?"

"I've already asked so much of her."

But Sheldon didn't seem to care. He grabbed Sebastian's hand and pulled him to his feet. "I want to talk to her about all of this, anyway. Come on."

Sebastian didn't want to leave Caven on his own, but when he looked at his mate, it was to find Caven and Cain talking over their lunch. When he leaned closer to tell Caven he'd be right back, Caven nodded and kissed him, then went back to his conversation right away.

He looked like he fit. It certainly looked like Cain had forgiven him or was in the process of doing so, and Sebastian hoped he was.

He allowed Sheldon to drag him down hallways until they

reached the throne room. He knew the palace by now, and he wasn't as intimidated as he'd been in the beginning. Two guards were standing by the doors, and Sheldon quickly talked to one of them. She disappeared into the room, only to reappear a few seconds later and nod.

Sheldon grinned and dragged Sebastian inside.

The queen was at the back of the room, at the small sitting area behind the curtains. She was having lunch, just like they'd been, but she smiled when she saw them. "Not that I mind having people with me for lunch, but you don't usually visit me at this time of day," she said.

Sheldon smiled at her. "Sorry to bother you, but Sebastian and I were talking about his problem."

"The man hunting him?"

"Yes. He already told me you greenlighted a team of dragons to threaten the guy and make sure he doesn't hurt anyone ever again, but we were wondering about Sebastian's family."

"What about them?" Ita gestured at them to sit down and turned on the couch so she could face them.

Sebastian was nervous, so he was glad Sheldon was taking the lead. He had known the queen much longer, and the clan was truly his home, while Sebastian was still trying to get used to everything and everyone.

"Well, with the baby coming soon, I asked Sebastian if his family was going to move in with the clan."

"It's not something Sebastian has asked me about," the queen said.

Sebastian cleared his throat. "I didn't want to bother anyone. I mean, you've already been so good to me. You gave me a home."

"But the queen wants more humans to live with the clan. Since she trusts you, she'll also trust your family, which is perfect."

"Is that what you want, Sebastian?" the queen asked. "Do

you want your family to be allowed to move in with the clan?"

"It would be perfect. I'm not sure all of them would come, but I'd like to make the offer. I also know that my grandfather and my father would be over the moon at the opportunity of being here when the baby is born."

The queen nodded. "I see. Well, I don't have a problem with them moving in. How many of you are there?"

Sebastian could hardly believe what was happening. "If everyone moves, it'll be four of them."

"That won't be a problem. We'll find rooms for them, although not in the royal wing. I'll ask servants to get them ready."

Sebastian blinked. "You mean they can move in right away?"

"I think it would be better for them to be here before the meeting, if they can manage. I'd rather not spare guards during the meeting, and unless you want to wait until it's over, I think this is the best thing to do for everyone. Call them and see what they say. I doubt you and Caven will want to travel to them, so I'll send a team. They'll reach your family in a few days, so they'll have plenty of time to pack their things."

Sebastian could have cried. "Why are you doing this?" he asked.

"Why not? As I already told you, I want humans and dragons to live together. I truly believe this is what we were meant to do. If it weren't, we wouldn't be having children together."

Whether or not she was right, Sebastian didn't care. The only thing he cared about was that soon he'd have his entire family gathered under the same roof.

He couldn't have been happier.

CHAPTER THIRTEEN

Sebastian looked around. "Are we really meeting in the middle of the forest?" he asked.

Caven nodded. "The humans have agreed."

"I know. It's just weird, I guess. When I think of this kind of meeting, I imagine they happen in offices, not between trees."

But that wasn't how dragons worked. Even when they had meetings between clans, they never held it in one of their homes. It would be too dangerous and make them too vulnerable. Just like the meeting of clans, they'd have this one in the middle of the forest so the humans wouldn't find out where the palace was.

The Ogorth clan had arrived a few days earlier. They'd immediately set up tents, and the guards had been patrolling since then. Everyone was tense, even though the area was safe. There was no way to be sure what the humans would do, even though the queen had already talked to the man they were meeting. It could be a trap, and the queen could be in danger.

But that was why they'd brought guards along. There were more than enough of them that the queen would be safe, and that was what Caven had to remember. He also had to remember that *he* was safe, too. Morven had assured him that they'd keep an eye on him, especially because of the pregnancy. For a moment, Caven had wondered if it was an excuse, but he was starting to realize that Morven would have told him. He just wanted to keep Caven safe, something that still puzzled Caven.

Sebastian leaned back in his chair. "It's still strange to me."

"You could always go home."

"I'm not going anywhere. The queen asked me to be here, and besides, since my family's been delayed, I don't have a reason to be at the palace right now."

They'd tried to get Sebastian's family to the palace in the days before the meeting, but they hadn't managed. Considering they had to quit jobs and pack up their apartments, it made sense. Hell, they had to pack up their *lives*. Sebastian's sister still wasn't sure she was coming, at least not for the long term, but she was excited to meet dragons and Sebastian's child.

They'd all be there with Sebastian. In the end, that was all that mattered, and once these meetings were over, Sebastian, Caven, Morven, and a few other dragons would head to the city to threaten Patrick O'Neill. Caven wished he could eat the human, but he'd been ordered to stay out of the fight, and he would. He was only going so he'd be there for Sebastian, and that was that.

"So, what's the plan?" Sebastian asked.

They were having breakfast by the tent they shared, but they needed to hurry. The human delegation was supposed to arrive at any moment. The guards would warn them when the humans got close, and Caven wanted to be ready when it happened.

He was nervous about the humans finding out about his pregnancy. Sebastian had told him that they'd probably think he was overweight, because most of the time, humans couldn't wrap their minds around things that worked differently from what they considered normal. Most human men couldn't get pregnant, so they wouldn't even think it was a possibility. Caven didn't like feeling this vulnerable, but his cousin had wanted him here, so here he was. At least he wasn't alone. Sebastian was with him, and he wasn't the only one.

Everyone was here, including Dagan, Slavin's mate. He still limped, but his legs were much better. He'd healed incredibly fast after his king had tortured him, and he'd wanted to be there to protect the queen. Even Sheldon and Blake had traveled with them. The queen wanted them and Sebastian to be present because she wanted humans to see that dragons and humans could live together. Sheldon had been grumpy about being away from the children, but they were safe back at the palace. Caven could understand wanting to stay with them, though. He'd tried to imagine how he'd feel if he had to leave his egg or his child behind, and he didn't like it.

"At least once this is over, we'll head to the city," Sebastian said.

"You're too eager to kick Patrick's ass," Caven pointed out with a smile.

"Aren't you? He could have killed me."

"But he didn't. Instead, he gave you this life."

Sebastian narrowed his eyes. "He's not the one who did that. If he'd been able to, he'd have killed me. You're the one who gave me this life." He leaned over the table and took one of Caven's hands. "And I wouldn't have it any other way."

It still flustered Caven when Sebastian talked to him like that, so he turned his attention back to his breakfast. A few minutes later, two guards burst into the small clearing created by the tents, and Caven knew the time had arrived.

As had the humans.

The guards made a beeline for Ita's tent, and Caven got to his feet to follow. Sebastian was next to him in seconds, helping him waddle through the clearing. As happy as Caven was about having this baby, he wouldn't miss feeling like he'd eaten a whole watermelon. His balance had changed, and sometimes he stumbled on air. Now he truly needed

Sebastian to stay by his side. He'd have taken a tumble a few times if Sebastian hadn't been there to keep him up.

One of the guards left the tent, pausing to let Caven and Sebastian pass. Caven wasn't surprised to see how the tent had been set up. Two areas were separated by curtains, and the front one held a long table with chairs.

The queen was already seated at the head of the table, and she warmly smiled when she saw Caven and Sebastian. "I hope you slept well?" she asked.

"I don't think I can sleep well at the moment," Caven grumbled as Sebastian helped him toward the table.

Ita gestured at one of the chairs right next to her. "Caven, sit with me. Sebastian, you can have the seat next to him. And yes, I remember my pregnancy well. It's not easy, is it?"

"I'm sure I'll miss it when it's over, but I can't wait to lay the egg for now."

"It'll happen soon. Just please, wait until we're back in the palace."

Sebastian laughed, but the sound had a hysterical edge. "Please, don't mention him giving birth here in the middle of the forest. I don't think I could stand it."

"It wouldn't be giving birth, exactly," Caven said.

"It would still be too close for comfort. Cain told me that he laid his egg in the forest, and it doesn't sound great."

Caven agreed, and he hoped his body would, too.

He sat in the chair, relieved he wouldn't have to do this on his feet. Maybe it would help hide his pregnancy, or maybe the humans would notice and ask questions. At this point, he wouldn't be surprised by anything, and it would be better to let Ita handle it. She knew what she was doing.

The table slowly filled. Sheldon and Blake sat in front of Caven and Sebastian. Sheldon was still grumpy and bitching that he really should have stayed home, but Ita smiled at him. She understood how hard it was to be away from her son better than anyone. Caven was ready to bet she didn't see Blue as often as she wanted to because of being queen. Blue spent a lot of time with Blake and Orran and not enough of it with his mother. Unfortunately, there wasn't much anyone could do to change that.

"They're here," Morven said, poking his head in at the entrance of the tent.

Ita nodded. "Bring them in."

Sebastian stilled next to Caven, and Caven took his hand under the table. He squeezed, silently trying to reassure his mate. Everything would be all right.

It had to be.

The sound of footsteps approaching made Caven sit straighter in his chair. He watched as one of the flaps of the tent was flipped up and the first human came in.

He was wearing some kind of uniform, which probably meant he was the envoy's guard. Another man dressed like him walked in, then a man dressed differently who must have been Gideon. He almost pushed the guards away in his rush to meet the queen.

From what Caven had observed, this man was eager to meet dragons. He'd seemed nice when he'd talked to Ita, and they were about to find out if he really was the good person he'd appeared to be during the video calls.

Gideon smiled widely. He stopped by the queen and bowed, something that surprised Caven. "Your Majesty," he said.

Ita got to her feet. "It's a pleasure to meet you in person, Gideon."

"The same goes for me. Shall we sit?"

"Let's start this meeting," Ita agreed.

Caven sucked in a breath. Whatever happened next, whatever the humans wanted, he had to remember it wouldn't change what he and Sebastian shared. Sebastian was in his life to stay, and he would, no matter what these humans said or wanted.

It was odd to be here. Sebastian still didn't fully understand why the queen had wanted him to be present during this meeting, but he'd stopped asking her. Every time he did, she told him it was because she wanted to show the human delegation that humans and dragons could live together. He supposed it made sense, yet at the same time, it didn't. It wasn't his job to worry about it, though, so he stayed where he was, sitting next to Caven, and he listened.

It was easy to understand who in the human delegation was a guard and who was here for the meetings. The guards wore uniforms, while Gideon and a few other people wore suits. There was even a woman in a skirt and heels, and Sebastian felt sorry for her having to walk on the roots and fallen leaves.

The humans sat at the other side of the table, with Gideon facing the queen. Sebastian saw his gaze stop on him, then quickly move on to Sheldon and Blake.

"I have to say I'm surprised to see there are humans on your side of the table," Gideon said.

The queen smiled at him. "I suppose you are. It was important to me that they were here today. These are Sebastian, Blake, and Sheldon," she said, pointing at them.

Sebastian stupidly raised a hand and waved, instantly regretting it. He wasn't a child, dammit.

"They're part of my clan, and all three of them are mated with clan dragons."

Gideon's eyes went round. "Are they? So it's something you allow?"

He was clearly making an effort not to stare at the dragons, but some of the other humans weren't as well behaved as he was. The woman stared openly at Morven, who was standing next to the queen, and one of the other two men couldn't seem to look away from Ita.

Sebastian could understand that. Dragons were fascinating, and the queen even more so. She had a presence to her, something that told everyone in the room that she was powerful. Sebastian had felt it in the beginning, too. He still did, even though he'd been seeing her quite often lately. She'd met with him, Sheldon, and Blake, wanting to know what to expect from Gideon and his people, and while Sebastian wouldn't say they were friends, she was more than the queen to him now.

"I firmly believe humans and dragons are meant to live together," the queen explained.

She didn't mention anything about the dragon-human children, which was just as well. Sebastian didn't want anyone to know about his child or Sheldon's. Unfortunately, when humans didn't understand something, they either shunned it or tried to experiment on it. No one here wanted to take that risk.

Gideon smiled and nodded. "It's why we're here, after all." He opened the folder of documents he'd brought with him. "Shall we get started?"

Sebastian tuned out after that. From what he could tell, the queen and Gideon went over some things they'd already talked about, and it was kind of boring. The queen gave Gideon a list of what she wanted for dragons, which included equal rights to those of humans, and Sebastian almost snorted. He wanted dragons to be equal to humans, but that would never happen. Humans weren't equal to humans most of the time.

But he had to have hope. Besides, as long as whatever happened meant he was safe with the clan, he didn't care. He doubted most dragons did, either. As far as he knew, they tended to stay with their clan rather than explore the human world, and he didn't blame them after what humans had done.

For decades, they'd hunted and killed dragons for sport and money. They'd used dragons' bodies to get rich, and even though they believed dragons were nothing more than animals, Sebastian was disgusted by their behavior. He wanted anyone who'd hurt a dragon again, even knowing they had a human form, to pay for it, but he was only here to show the humans that dragons and humans could be together. He didn't have a say in the conversations happening around the table, and that was perfectly fine.

Gideon gestured at the documents in front of him. "However, as I told you during our calls, it can take a long time for new laws to be created. Most of the country supports these laws, but I won't deny that others have been campaigning against them."

"Do you think they'll pass?" Sheldon asked.

Gideon seemed stunned to have one of the humans talk to him. Sebastian almost laughed, but he was interested in what Sheldon was asking. Even though he had no plans to leave the clan, he wanted to know that Caven and their child would be safe, whatever happened next. He wanted all the dragons to be safe.

Except maybe Caven's father. He wouldn't mind handing him over to the human government for them to experiment on, to be honest.

"Eventually," Gideon confirmed. "And in the meantime, we're keeping an eye on the hunters. There's been a lot of talk from them lately, which makes sense. They're trying to spin what happened to their advantage, and they don't want to appear as monsters who killed human beings. I'm not saying everything will go quickly and smoothly, but we're doing everything we can."

Blake leaned over the table. "Why?"

Gideon blinked at him. "I'm sorry?"

"Why are you doing this? Knowing what I do about the government, I'm kind of surprised you're not trying to use dragons in some way. Even though dragons are powerful, they're a minority, and you're very much aware of that."

Gideon stared at Blake for a moment. His focus moved around the table, but he quickly turned his attention back to Blake. "I can only tell you what I know."

"I don't expect you to tell me what you don't know," Blake said with humor in his voice.

"Dragons might be a minority, but if there was a war between dragons and humans, even if dragons lost, they could inflict a lot of damage to us and our society. We don't want that to happen. On the other hand, dragons could be important allies if we treat them right."

It made sense. When dragons were in their dragon form, they were almost invincible. Sebastian wasn't surprised the government wanted to take advantage of that.

"That's what we're aiming for," the queen agreed.

Gideon nodded. He was almost bouncing in his seat, and it was endearing to see. Sebastian wouldn't have trusted any other envoy, but he did trust Gideon. He realized that was probably dangerous, and maybe Gideon was behaving this way on purpose, but he didn't think so.

"We've compiled a list of hunters we were able to identify. Some of them were present during the attack on your clan, and while we can't arrest them, we're watching them. They'll be behind bars as soon as they do something they shouldn't do, and dragons won't have to worry about them ever again. We'll also warn dragons if we find out hunters are planning anything." Gideon hesitated. "And while I know it's not right for dragons to hide away, I think that at least in the beginning, it would be better if all of you stayed home within your clans. Humans should still see you, maybe using social media, because they need to know that you're human, too. But I'm afraid it would be too dangerous for dragons to start mixing with humans just yet."

Sebastian remembered how shocked he'd been when Caven had shifted in front of him. He agreed that humans needed to see that so they were ready for it, but also that they shouldn't see it from up close. It would be too easy for someone to freak out and attack, and that was the last thing anyone around the table wanted.

Caven shifted in his seat, and Sebastian turned his attention to him. Caven seemed absorbed in what Gideon was saying, but he must have felt Sebastian staring at him. He quickly turned and smiled at Sebastian.

Sebastian smiled back. As far as he was concerned, whatever the queen and Gideon decided, he'd be okay with it. He had no intention of leaving the clan ever again, anyway. There was nothing out there for him in the human world, not once his family moved in with the clan. The palace was full of people important to him, though, and that was all he wanted to focus on. His family, Caven, and their baby.

Their future.

"What about punishments for the humans who hurt dragons from now on?" Caven asked.

He didn't want to draw attention, but he felt this needed to be asked. The others had asked intelligent questions, and Caven was glad to have the answers, but he was still worried. All through dragons' history, humans had been hunting them. Caven doubted that would change just because they now knew dragons had a human form, and he wanted whoever hurt another dragon to pay for it. However, that would only work if the human government went along with it. Caven wouldn't be surprised if they refused, but it was central to the Ogorth clan's decision.

They couldn't ally themselves with humans if humans treated them as if they were no better than animals.

Gideon linked his fingers together as he turned his attention to Caven. "I realize that humans have been allowed to hurt and kill dragons in the past. They won't be anymore. We can't do anything about what happened before, but this is one of the laws that are being passed."

"And in the meantime? Because you said it would take a while for the laws to be passed. What will happen to the hunters who kill dragons as we're waiting?"

"I understand you're worried, and I promise we're working on something that will be quicker. Even if it's only temporary, it'll be enough to fill the gap until a definitive law is put in place."

Caven leaned forward. "What about our eggs? Will they have the same rights?"

Gideon looked startled, but only for a second. "We'll regard them as children. As far as we're concerned, they're your offspring, whether or not they're born yet. I realize how much money hunters can get for an egg on the black market. We've been working on shutting them down, and while I doubt we'll find all of them, we're trying. The situation is never going to be perfect from either side."

Caven rested back in his chair and pressed his hands to his stomach. Gideon wasn't wrong. They'd never have perfection, but that didn't mean dragons should accept whatever humans were ready to throw at them. They needed equal rights, and they needed hunters to be punished when they hurt dragons.

"I hope you're right," Ita said. "Because if humans don't punish the criminals, dragons will. If we're attacked, we'll defend ourselves, and as you said earlier, it won't end well. Humans might win, but we'll take as many of them out as we can before we go."

Gideon paled. It was good that he understood Ita wasn't making an empty promise. She meant every word she said, and the humans needed to be aware of that.

"We'll do everything we can to keep the dragons safe," Gideon promised. "But we can't control every single human. I have no doubt that there will be accidents, and I apologize in advance for them, but there's nothing more than we're already doing that we can do to stop them."

Ita stared at him for a moment. She looked every bit the queen she was, and Caven was proud. He'd been an idiot to think he could take her place on the throne, but never again. Never again would he go along with what his father wanted.

"I suppose that promises are the only thing we can give each other at the moment," she said. "I believe we're going in the right direction, though. We both want to avoid a war and the bloodshed that would come with it."

Gideon nodded eagerly. "We do. I realize you don't trust me, and I don't blame you for that. But I can promise you that as long as I'm on your side, you won't have to worry about a thing. I'll always try to protect dragons."

For some reason, Caven believed him. Still, Gideon wasn't in charge of the country. As many promises as he could make, he might not be able to keep them, no matter how hard he tried.

But that went for everyone. The queen promised that dragons wouldn't attack humans, but she couldn't control every dragon. Caven wouldn't be surprised if Bergen became a problem, and unfortunately, there was no way to prevent it. They'd have to deal with Bergen and his clan when Bergen acted, and in the meantime, they could do nothing but wait.

Caven hated waiting.

CHAPTER FOURTEEN

Caven was exhausted, but unfortunately for him, he wasn't done even though the meeting was over. Now that dragons and humans had agreed on what each of them would do, it was time to turn his attention to Patrick O'Neill.

He'd tried to kill Sebastian. He'd almost taken away Caven's future, and even though Sebastian was far away from O'Neill now, he was still terrified. Caven didn't like it. He wanted Sebastian to be nothing but happy, especially since they were about to have a child together. That meant getting rid of O'Neill, and while Caven couldn't physically take part in the next step, he'd be there to watch.

He hoped O'Neill was so terrified he'd run away screaming.

"Everyone ready?" Sheldon asked.

He sounded way too gleeful for what was about to happen, and Caven still wasn't sure why he'd insisted on coming along. "I thought you'd want to go back to the clan as soon as possible," he said.

Sheldon grinned. "I do, but I want to be part of this. My daughter is safe with the clan, but Sebastian isn't, and I want that to change."

Sheldon and Sebastian had grown close over the past few weeks. Caven had been glad to see it, just like he'd been glad to realize that he was making friends, too. He could hardly believe it, but the dragon he was closest to was Cain. Even though Caven had grown up in the royal family, he and Cain shared a past of abuse they'd bonded over. Caven wasn't sure

148

Cain had entirely forgiven him for what he'd done, but he was on the path to doing so.

Along with his acceptance had come the acceptance of everyone else. Hogan still kept his distance from Caven, but Caven didn't blame him. He'd almost lost everything because of Caven, and it was a miracle he hadn't tried to kill him the first time he'd found him and Cain talking.

Caven was glad he hadn't.

"We want Sebastian's family to be safe," Blake said, hooking an arm around Sebastian's shoulders. "They're our family now."

Caven could understand that. The clan was made up of many small related groups, but in the end, they were all a big family who cared for each other. He was sure that the fact that Sheldon, Blake, and Sebastian were the only humans until Sebastian's family arrived had pushed them close together, but why they'd become friends didn't matter. The only thing that did was that now, they were important to each other and that Sheldon and Blake wanted to help Sebastian.

"I researched the asshole," Sheldon began. "And honestly, I'll be glad once he's behind bars. What he did to that poor woman was only the tip of the iceberg. He needs to pay, if not for her murder, for everything else. He should spend the rest of his life in jail."

If Caven had been hesitant about confronting O'Neill, he would have changed his mind by now. The man deserved whatever was coming at him, and while they'd promised Ita they'd try not to kill him, Caven wasn't too sure he'd step in if someone lost control. He supposed they'd see what happened once they were with O'Neill.

"It's time to go?" Sebastian asked.

He sounded hesitant, but Caven suspected it was more because he hadn't seen O'Neill since the night O'Neill had tried to kill him than because he was afraid. He knew he'd be protected by the group of dragons coming with him. Nothing would happen to him, not this time.

Caven shifted, relieved to be able to spend time in his dragon body. It was easier for him to carry the egg in this form, and he would have spent the last part of his pregnancy as a dragon if Sebastian hadn't been human. As it was, it wouldn't be fair to Sebastian not to be able to talk to him, so Caven was pushing on. He only had a few weeks to wait, anyway.

He stretched out his wings, then his neck. Once he was done, he looked expectantly at Sebastian. Caven had carried him to the spot where they'd met the humans, so Sebastian was getting used to riding him in his dragon form. He climbed on after placing the harness he and the other humans used to ride their dragon on Caven's back, and then they were off.

It still felt good and freeing to be flying, but not as much as before. Now, Caven was free even when he was home, and being in his dragon form didn't hold the same emotions. It held different ones, though. He could share this with Sebastian, which was incredible.

Caven followed the others in the air. Morven was carrying Sheldon, and while Orran had gone back to the palace with the queen, Hogan was there, and he was carrying Blake. Slavin and his mate were present, too, and they'd seemed eager to help. Hopefully, so many dragons would be enough to scare O'Neill into giving himself up to the police, but Caven wouldn't hold his breath. O'Neill didn't strike him as the kind of man who would do something that wouldn't benefit him.

They'd waited until night fell, and since they'd had the meeting with Gideon as far as possible from the palace, it only took a handful of hours of flight. When they reached the city, it was the middle of the night. The city was never silent, as Caven had learned during the time he'd lived there, but it was a safe bet to think that O'Neill was asleep. Sheldon had found his address, and once they reached it, they landed on the roof.

Do we know if he's alone? Morven asked through the mental bond all dragons shared.

I'll shift and go downstairs to grab him. Hogan turned back to his human form and stretched. "I think the rest of you should stay in your dragon form. I'll grab him and drag him up to the roof, and he'll freak out when he sees so many dragons."

Slavin shifted, too. "Good idea, but I'm coming with you."

Caven was relieved he wouldn't have to shift again. He felt Sebastian climb off his back, but he didn't go far. He leaned against Caven's side, his body almost vibrating with nerves. Caven couldn't tell him everything would be okay since they couldn't communicate in this form, but he rubbed his muzzle against Sebastian's head.

Sebastian laughed. "You've messed up my hair, haven't you?"

Caven had, and just to be on the safe side, he gave Sebastian's hair a lick. Sebastian yelped and pushed Caven's head away, but he was laughing.

"That was awful," he said, wagging his finger at Caven.

Caven grinned, exposing his fangs. Anyone else would have been terrified, but not Sebastian.

Never Sebastian.

Raised voices made everyone turn toward the entrance of the roof. Hogan had left the door open, but Caven would have been able to hear the shrill voice of the terrified human even with the door closed.

It looked like Hogan and Slavin had found Patrick O'Neill.

The sound of footsteps came closer, and Caven raised one of his wings. He draped it over Sebastian's back, even though it was a bit heavy and Sebastian's knees buckled. Sebastian didn't protest. He moved even closer to Caven as if he were afraid O'Neill would hurt him.

Not on Caven's watch.

The human suddenly appeared at the open door. He stumbled forward, probably because Hogan had pushed him and landed on his knees. He was only wearing a pair of boxers, and his pale skin gleamed under the moonlight. His hair was wild, and his eyes were wide as he looked around and took in the scene in which he'd just appeared.

Three humans stood there, but that wasn't what grabbed O'Neill's attention. No, that was the three dragons glaring at him.

Caven grinned. They had no plans of killing O'Neill, but it didn't mean they couldn't have fun with him.

Sebastian tried to imagine the scene from Patrick's point of view. He supposed he'd be terrified, too, if he was pulled out of his bed in the middle of the night by dragons, then confronted by three more on the roof. Sebastian wasn't afraid of dragons, but Patrick *really* was.

"Who the fuck are you?" Patrick demanded to know. "What do you want from me? You can't do this."

Hogan and Slavin stayed silent. They looked at Caven and Sebastian for guidance, but Sebastian had no idea what to do. The plan had been to come here and threaten Patrick until he gave himself up to the cops and stayed out of Sebastian's life, but Sebastian wasn't sure it was a good idea anymore. He didn't know if he could do this.

Still, he was here. He might as well show Patrick what he'd be going against if he tried hurting him again.

He gently pushed away Caven's wing and stepped out from under it. Patrick's head snapped toward him, and Sebastian sucked in a breath. Whatever happened, whatever Patrick tried to do, he'd never touch Sebastian again. The dragons standing around them would make sure of that.

They'd decided Caven would stay in his dragon form so Patrick wouldn't notice he was pregnant, but now, Sebastian wished Caven could speak for him. He was much better with words than Sebastian had ever been.

"Remember me?" he asked.

"How can I ever forget you?" Patrick spat out. "You ruined my life."

Sebastian snorted. "*I* ruined *your* life? You killed a woman. You tried to kill me. As far as I can see, you've been doing everything on your own, including threatening me."

"What the fuck do you want?"

"It's simple. I want you to leave me alone."

"Fine."

"I'm not done."

Patrick had been getting to his feet, but Hogan put a hand on his shoulder and pushed him back down. Patrick tried to act brave, but Sebastian could see he was terrified.

He didn't blame him. It would be easy for any of the dragons in their dragon form to eat Patrick in one bite. They wouldn't, because apparently, humans didn't taste right, especially when they were wearing clothes, but Patrick didn't know that. If he hadn't talked to dragons and gotten to know them, Sebastian wouldn't have, either.

"You'll go to the cops," Sebastian continued. He dared take a step away from Caven, but Caven grumbled and used his wing to draw him back. He was being overprotective, and Sebastian was fine staying where he was.

"I can't go to the cops," Patrick protested. He eyed Hogan nervously, but Hogan didn't move.

"You can, and you will. You'll confess to every crime you ever committed in your life, including the murder of that poor woman. You'll plead guilty for everything, and you'll spend the rest of your life in jail."

"I can't —"

"You can if you don't want one of these dragons to kill you," Sebastian said, making his voice as hard as possible. "Everyone thinks dragons are monsters, but in reality, it's humans who are. You're one of the worst, and if you don't agree to go to the police and actually do it, one of these dragons will come back and kill you. Would that be better for you, Patrick? Do you want to die, or would you rather spend the rest of your life in jail?"

It was clear Patrick didn't want to say yes, but he didn't have a choice. Sebastian doubted any of the dragons would actually come back and kill Patrick even if he didn't go to the police, but Patrick didn't know that. Even Hogan, who was a fierce protector and fighter, wouldn't kill a human in cold blood.

But he certainly looked like he might.

Patrick's gaze moved from Hogan to the dragons, stopping on Caven. "If I do that, you'll keep them away from me?"

"I will," Sebastian confirmed. "You'll never see these dragons again, or me, for that matter."

"Fine. I'll do it."

"You'll do it now. Go downstairs, get dressed, and head out. We'll keep an eye on you until we're sure you did what you said you'd do."

Patrick was only too happy to get out of there. Sebastian watched him as he scrambled through the door and almost fell down the stairs. He wasn't going to follow Patrick to the police station. Sebastian could easily find out if Patrick had kept his promise, and if the man hadn't, the dragons would be back.

The thought made Sebastian smile. He was safe, and his family was safe.

And they were about to move in with the clan.

That was the other reason they were here. Since they'd planned on being in the city, anyway, they'd decided to pick up Sebastian's family. They were ready, even Sebastian's sister. She'd been reassured when Sebastian had told her that she could get a job with the dragons and was more than happy to move in with the clan.

They would all be there, with Sebastian, and he'd never have to worry about them ever again. Even if something happened to him, he knew the clan would keep his family safe. They'd be clan members, just like every dragon who belonged with the clan, and they'd be safer than they could ever be on their own in the city.

Sebastian couldn't wait to hug his dad and grandfather and for all of them to meet Caven. Then, in a few weeks, Caven would lay the egg, and Sebastian would be there with him. It would still take time before the egg was ready to hatch, but that was fine.

Now Sebastian had all the time in the world. There was no one after him anymore, and he could dedicate his life to making Caven happy.

He grinned as he turned to Caven, ready to climb onto his back again. It was time to get his family and go home.

Caven could almost feel Sebastian vibrating on his back. It made him smile, and at the same time, he was worried. Sebastian's family was important to him, so important that he'd asked the queen to have them live with the clan. What would happen if they didn't like Caven?

It wouldn't be because he was a dragon. They seemed happy enough to move in with the clan, and they'd have to deal with many dragons there. But they'd eventually hear what he'd done, and they'd judge him for it. He wouldn't blame them if they did, but he didn't want Sebastian and his family to have a falling out because of him. He didn't think Sebastian would break up with him, especially not with the baby coming, but he might lose his family because of what Caven had done.

Caven would never forgive himself if that happened.

But there was no going back. Sebastian was excited about getting his family moved into the palace, and they were headed to pick them up now. The trip home would be a long one, and they'd have to stop at least twice to rest during the day, possibly three times. Caven would have plenty of time to show Sebastian's family how important Sebastian was to him and that he'd do everything in his power to make Sebastian happy.

I can almost hear you thinking, Morven said.

It took Caven a moment to realize he was talking to him. *I'm sorry?*

You're nervous. You're about to meet Sebastian's parents, so it makes sense.

It did make sense, but Morven didn't fully understand. He'd never met Sheldon's parents, and from what Caven had heard, it was a good thing he hadn't. *What if they don't like me? What if they don't want me to be with Sebastian?*

They'll love you.

Hogan snorted loudly enough for Caven to hear him, even at a distance. Caven almost laughed, and not because Hogan was being rude. Caven felt the way Hogan did, and he doubted anyone would love him. Well, anyone but Sebastian.

You're not helping, Morven scolded Hogan. *I'm trying to re-assure Caven here.*

You'll be fine, Dagan intervened.

Of all of them, he was probably the one who understood Caven best. He and his family had recently moved in with the clan, and he'd met Slavin's family. Of course, he'd been badly wounded when he had, and they'd fussed over him, but maybe the pregnancy would work the same way for Caven.

A small hand patted Caven's back. He didn't turn around to look at Sebastian because he didn't want them to fall out of the sky, but he grunted so Sebastian knew he was listening to him.

"What's the bunch of you talking about?" Sebastian asked. "Because I know you're talking about something. It's obvious, and it's making me nervous."

It wasn't like Caven could explain, so he grunted again.

Whatever happened, he supposed he was about to find out, and he'd deal with it. He wouldn't have a choice if he wanted to be in Sebastian's life, and he did. He wouldn't let anything or anyone take Sebastian from him, and if it meant he had to make Sebastian's family love him, he would. It wouldn't have worked if he'd still been the dragon his father wanted him to be, but now, he was different. Even if they didn't love him, he didn't think they'd dislike him so much that they'd demand Sebastian break up with him.

Caven prayed that wouldn't happen.

"It's that building over there," Sebastian said.

Caven felt him shift on his back, and he hoped Sebastian wouldn't slide off. It wouldn't be the best introduction to Sebastian's family to drop him while they were flying.

But they were there, so Caven slowly lowered to the roof of the building. It was an apartment complex similar to the one where Sebastian had lived before, and most of the windows of the building were dark. There was a light on the roof, though, and once they got close enough, Caven realized it was a flashlight. Sebastian's family was waiting for them, and they were telling them they saw them.

Caven took the lead, since he was carrying Sebastian. He landed first, keeping a good distance between them and Sebastian's family so they wouldn't get hurt by a flailing wing or slipping foot. He was just folding his wings around him when a young man who looked remarkably like Sebastian tried to climb him in his haste to get to Sebastian.

"I'm going to kill you when I get my hands on you!" he

said.

Caven was alarmed for a second, but thankfully, Sebastian patted his back as he slid off. "Christian is kidding. He's not going to hurt me." Sebastian turned to look at his cousin. "Do you really need to threaten me with death in front of my mate?"

Christian threw himself into Sebastian's arms. Caven was unsure what to do, but the most polite thing would be for him to shift so Sebastian could introduce him to his family. So, he did, but he kept his distance as two more people rushed closer and threw themselves at Sebastian and Christian, who were hugging. A fourth person was slower to move toward them, but he wrapped his arms around them when he reached them.

Sebastian was back where he belonged.

Caven watched, a smile on his lips. This was all he'd wanted for Sebastian. He didn't deserve to be kept away from his family, especially for something as wrong as being hunted because he'd seen a man kill someone. Now, Sebastian was safe, and he always would be. He was reunited with his family, and Caven knew that he had everything he'd ever needed as far as he was concerned.

"Come on, guys," he heard Sebastian murmur. "I'm fine. I promise I am. Caven and the clan kept me safe."

The only woman of their little group reached out and punched Sebastian's arm none too gently. "You disappeared for weeks, and we didn't know if you were safe."

"I called you several times. I *showed* you I was safe."

"Yeah, but we hadn't seen you with our own eyes. How would you have felt if I'd vanished suddenly, then I called you to tell you *hey, I'm safe and now living with dragons, and there's a guy trying to kill me, but don't worry about me?*"

Sebastian laughed. "Okay, you've got me there. But I really am fine." He turned and held a hand out, and Caven did the only thing he could.

He took Sebastian's hand and allowed him to pull him closer.

"Everyone, this is Caven, my mate." Sebastian stepped next to Caven and wrapped an arm around his waist. The movement drew attention to Caven's stomach, and he watched as everyone's eyes widened.

"I know you said he was pregnant, but I didn't expect this," Christian murmured.

Sebastian rolled his eyes. "What did you expect? He's pregnant, so of course it shows."

"He's a guy."

"So?" Sebastian's sister asked. "Some human men can get pregnant, too, so I don't see what's extraordinary about this. I mean, the pregnancy is the least interesting thing about Caven." She stepped forward and offered Caven her hand. "It's a pleasure to meet you. I'm Jayna."

Caven took her hand and squeezed it. Shaking it didn't feel like the right thing to do. "It truly is a pleasure to meet you," he said, slightly bowing his head. He looked around. "It's a pleasure to meet all of you. Sebastian has told me so much about you that it feels as if I already know you."

He let go of Jayna's hand and turned toward the other three. From what Sebastian and the clan humans had told him, he'd expected Sebastian's family to be wary. For one, they'd never seen a dragon in their human form until recently, and they certainly had never seen one from up close. Then there was the pregnancy. It wasn't just that Caven was a male yet was pregnant. It was also that Sebastian, the cousin and brother and son they loved, was about to become a father.

The older man stepped forward and grabbed Caven's hand. "Since my grandson isn't introducing the rest of the family, let me do it for him. I'm Hyde, and this is my son, William. He's Sebastian's father. The last one is Christian, my daughter's son and Sebastian's cousin."

He didn't mention why Christian had been living with them or why he was coming along, but Caven already knew that story.

He forced himself to smile at all of them. It still felt awkward, so he was glad when Morven stepped closer.

"Good evening," he said. "I'm Morven, and I'm the queen's head of security. Are you ready to go? Because the night won't be much longer, and I'd like for us to be as far away from the city as possible once the sun rises."

Christian was staring at the dragons around him with wide eyes and a slightly open mouth, but Jayna and the rest of the family didn't seem as fascinated or intimidated as he was. She smiled and nodded, then stepped back to grab a backpack. She swung it over her shoulders, then looked at the other bags at her feet.

"We tried to pack as light as possible," she said. "But it's not as easy as it sounds."

"Don't worry," Morven reassured her. "With so many of us, we'll be able to carry everything back to the palace."

They got to work. Thankfully, Sebastian's family *had* packed lightly, so they weren't bringing too many things. Soon enough, they were ready to go, and Caven was relieved to be able to shift back in his dragon form. The sky was already turning slightly lighter, which meant they wouldn't have much longer.

Sebastian clambered onto Caven's back, then patted his skin. "I'm ready to go."

Caven grunted and opened his wings. This was it. Once they were back at the palace, Caven doubted he'd ever return to the human world. Why would he when he had the best human by his side and in his nest?

Sebastian's heart felt like it was about to explode. It was an odd sensation, but he loved it and what it meant.

He looked around the clearing. His family was settled around him, huddled together as if they were afraid he'd disappear again. They were all asleep, and while he'd wanted to stretch out next to Caven, he'd understood his family's need to be close to him. So he'd agreed to lie down with them, but he wiggled close to Caven now that they were asleep.

Caven was in his dragon form. Cain had told Sebastian that it was more comfortable during the late stage of the pregnancy, so Sebastian was glad. He knew Caven was usually in his human form because he wanted them to be together and for Sebastian to understand him, and while he was touched, he also wanted Caven to be comfortable. If this was what it took, then he'd be more than happy to continue talking to Caven even though he couldn't respond. It wouldn't be for long, anyway.

Caven opened one eye when he felt Sebastian move against him. He raised his wing, and Sebastian snuggled under it, pressing his stomach against Caven's side. When Caven lowered his wing, it created a dark pocket of peace that made Sebastian sigh in pleasure.

He rubbed his cheek against Caven's side. The skin was smooth and warm, and even though Caven was in his dragon form, it smelled of him. It was soothing and reassuring, and Sebastian found himself feeling drowsy almost right away.

"I love you," Sebastian said.

It probably wasn't the best place or moment to tell Caven that for the first time, but Sebastian wanted Caven to know how he felt. If it weren't for the dragon, he wouldn't be here with his family. He'd be dead, his body rotting in that abandoned building. Instead, he was the happiest he'd ever been, and it was all thanks to Caven.

Caven's entire body jerked, so Sebastian patted his side. "Don't worry about saying it back. I don't expect you to, and it's not why I told you. I told you because it's how I feel. I love you, and I'm so glad we found each other."

To Sebastian's surprise, Caven's body rippled. One moment, Caven was a dragon. The next, he was in his human form, and his stomach was an obstacle between them.

Sebastian looked down at it and laughed. "You're beautiful when you're pregnant, but I kind of wish it was easier to kiss you," he said.

Caven grabbed him and dragged him closer. "I love you too," he said.

Sebastian beamed. "Good. It would've been awkward if you'd felt differently."

Caven chuckled, but it was wobbly and watery. He buried his face against Sebastian's neck as well as he could, considering his stomach, and Sebastian held him and listened to the sounds of the forest.

He could hear Hogan in his dragon form, keeping watch. Everyone else was asleep, and his grandfather was snoring. It was a surprise he wasn't keeping everyone awake, but Sebastian supposed they were all exhausted. They'd flown for the rest of the night, then a few hours in the early morning, and of course, there was everything that had come before reaching his family. They still had a few days of travel waiting for them, but they'd all be home by the end of it, and Sebastian would never have to leave the palace again.

He was looking forward to that.

He rubbed Caven's back, marveling at the difference between the smooth human skin and the slightly rougher dragon skin he could feel there. It wasn't a bad sensation. It was just different, and as Sebastian had learned recently, different was good.

"I can't believe you love me," Caven muttered against Sebastian's neck.

"Well, you better believe it. I love you and our baby, and

you're never getting rid of me."

Sebastian didn't know how to convince Caven of that. He understood why Caven was so bewildered by his affirmation, and he supposed that only time would make Caven see that Sebastian truly wasn't going anywhere. Caven had never been loved as a child or even as an adult, and he had no idea how to deal with having people who cared about him in his life.

Sebastian would teach him.

"You were a revelation," Caven murmured.

Sebastian shook his head. "I think that was you. You kept so much of yourself hidden away, and I know why you did it. It was necessary for you to survive what your father was pushing you to do. You never allowed anyone close, at least not until I arrived."

"And now, I have an entire family, and it's all thanks to you."

"In part. In part, it's because of you. You apologized. You explained what you did and why you did it, and in the end, people started seeing you the way I do. Now that they do, they can't stop themselves from loving you."

Caven hesitated. "What about your family? What do they think of me?"

Sebastian smiled. He'd suspected that was a worry Caven had, and he'd been waiting for him to ask. "Like I told you, they love you."

"They barely know me."

"Maybe, but *I* love you, and that's enough for them to love you. They want me to be happy, and they can see that I am when I'm with you. Besides, my sister said you were hot."

Caven's cheeks darkened, which made Sebastian laugh. He buried his face against Caven's chest, breathing him in. Caven's stomach was still between them, and while Sebastian couldn't feel the baby kicking, it didn't matter. He knew the baby was there, and Caven was in his arms. What more could he want from life?

"I can't wait for you to lay the egg," he whispered.

"Even when I do, it will be a while before the baby is born," Caven warned as if Sebastian didn't already know that.

"Doesn't matter. I'll be able to help you with that part, which is all I want. I don't like seeing you in discomfort or pain."

Caven sighed heavily, and his entire body sagged against Sebastian's. "Thank you," he whispered.

"I love you." Sebastian would never get tired of saying it, or of hearing it from Caven.

"I love you, too," Caven said.

He was falling asleep, and so was Sebastian, but that was okay. They'd have the rest of their lives to talk and say I love you.

EPILOGUE

Caven's entire body hurt. It didn't make sense, because his entire body wasn't involved in laying the egg, but that was what it felt like.

"You're doing great," the healer said. He smiled at Caven, but Caven could barely focus on him, let alone answer him.

"Is all of this normal?" Sebastian asked from Caven's side.

Caven squeezed Sebastian's hand. He reminded himself that Sebastian was human and that he had to be careful so he wouldn't hurt him, but Sebastian was entirely focused on Lisha.

"It's entirely normal," Lisha confirmed.

Caven had come to trust Lisha over the length of his pregnancy, and he knew he wouldn't lie to Sebastian. It was reassuring, but it didn't help with the pain.

Another contraction raked through Caven's body, and he tensed. He tried to breathe through it as Sebastian had taught him, but he felt it was impossible. How could he focus on anything that wasn't the pain?

"It's weird," Sebastian said.

Caven narrowed his eyes at him, but he didn't say anything. Sebastian was staring at the pouch on Caven's stomach. It was opening, and Caven could already see a sliver of a lightly colored egg. It was slick with the fluids helping with the laying and a little blood, but it was coming.

Lisha turned to Caven. "You're almost there, I promise."

"You promised I was almost there half an hour ago," Caven said through gritted teeth.

"I wasn't lying. Half an hour is nothing."

Caven wanted to shake him. From where he was, half an hour felt like an eternity.

He did as Lisha ordered when the next contraction came and gently pushed forward with his stomach muscles. He felt the egg slide, then something in his stomach popped. Sebastian made a strangled sound, and Caven looked down to see if something had gone wrong.

But nothing had. The egg was sliding out, and Lisha had wrapped both of his hands around it. He gently helped, and Caven couldn't look away.

Even with the fluids and the blood, he could see the egg was a light blue. It reflected both him and Sebastian, and Caven's chest felt full at that moment.

It would be a while before the egg hatched, but he and Sebastian were parents.

Lisha turned to the side and handed the egg to a second healer who was waiting for it. Caven couldn't look away as Myra gently dipped the egg into a bucket of warm water. He could feel Lisha working on him, touching his pouch, but he didn't care. His egg was there, getting cleaned, and he wanted to get his hands on it and never let go.

"I don't have words for what just happened," Sebastian said. He sounded like he was in shock, and when Caven turned to him, he realized he probably was.

He'd been by Caven's side the entire time. Caven had been woken up in the middle of the night by contractions, and he hadn't been surprised. Baby dragons always seemed to arrive during the night. Sebastian had been frantic, but he hadn't wavered. Now, he sat there, his blond curls all over the place and his green eyes wide. He was a little pale, which made his freckles more obvious, and Caven wondered what he could say to make him feel better.

"Sebastian?" he asked.

Sebastian blinked and looked at him. "Sorry. I guess it just hit that we have a baby."

"Well, it'll be several weeks before you have a baby," Lisha said. "But congratulations. You have an egg."

"That's one part of this that I have no idea what to expect of," Sebastian said with a grimace. "Sheldon told me a lot about this, but I forgot everything."

Lisha laughed. "You'll get it back. You're in shock, but it'll pass." He looked at Caven. "The pouch is already closing, and while you'll be sore for a few days, everything is as it should be. I'll visit you again at the end of the week, if that's okay with you."

Caven nodded, but his attention was on the egg again. Myra was done washing it, and she was wrapping it in a warm blanket. As soon as Caven's legs were steady, he'd get up to wash up, but for now, he was more than happy to stay in his nest.

Lisha patted Caven's knee and withdrew from the nest. Myra stepped forward, and when she held out the egg, Caven took it as if it were a fragile treasure.

And it was. The child he and Sebastian had created together was in there, getting ready to be born. A healer specialized in children and eggs would be here soon, but in the meantime, Sebastian and Caven had some time to be together.

Caven turned to the side and placed the egg between them in the nest. Sebastian mirrored his position, and both of them pressed a hand against the egg. It was warm and smooth, and Caven could have sworn he felt something move inside.

"This is so odd," Sebastian murmured.

A knock on the door interrupted whatever he'd been about to add. Sebastian shot to his feet, glaring at Caven when Caven started sitting up. He pointed his finger at him, then at the nest, silently ordering him to stay where he was.

That was perfectly fine with Caven.

Sebastian went to open the door. Caven could hear him speak, but he didn't look up until he heard footsteps by the nest. When he did, it was to find his cousin standing there.

This time, he sat up, no matter how hard Sebastian glared at him. "Ita. How did you know?"

"I know everything that happens in this palace," she said with a smile. "I was told by the guards that your contractions started during the night. I wanted to come by to see how you were doing, and I'm glad to see it's over."

"It wasn't the best experience," Caven admitted.

Her smile widened. "I remember it well. But Lisha assured me that both you and the egg are perfectly fine."

"And they need rest," Sebastian said a bit testily.

Thankfully, Ita didn't seem to mind. "I'll leave as quickly as possible. I just have something to say to Caven." She turned toward him. "I wanted to tell you that I'm happy you got out of your father's claws. I realize we haven't talked about what your father has been planning yet, and that we'll need to do it soon, but I'm glad to have you with me. I feel like this is how we were always supposed to work. I'm a stronger queen with you by my side, and once you've recuperated from the laying, I'd like to make your role as one of my advisors official."

Caven sucked in a breath. Kings and queens had several advisors, people they hand-picked for the role. Those advisors were dragons the queen trusted with her life—with her child's life. Some leaders had a lot of them, but it was an important role for Ita. She wouldn't give it to just anyone, and she hadn't. So far, the only advisors she had were Morven, Orran, and Sheldon.

Caven still remembered his father's face when she'd announced that she was taking a human as her advisor. He thought of that moment when he needed to be cheered up.

"I'd be delighted to accept the position," he said. "But are you sure? Most of the clan still doesn't trust me, and there's my father to deal with."

She waved Caven's words away. "You already know I don't care what the clan thinks. I am the queen, and that's not going to change. Eventually, they'll realize you're the perfect choice if they haven't already. As for your father, I won't deny that part of the reason I'm asking you to be my advisor is that your father will be bothered by it. I wonder if we can make his head explode with anger?"

Caven laughed. "Unfortunately, I don't think so. I've been trying for years." He got quieter. "But thank you. I would never have thought any of this could happen."

"It wouldn't have if you hadn't changed and if I hadn't finally been able to see the real you. I'm sorry I wasn't there for you when I should have been. What your father did to you isn't right, and I'll make sure he pays, one way or another."

But for now, it was dangerous to go after him, and that was perfectly fine with Caven. After all, he had plenty of other things to focus on, and his father wasn't going anywhere. Caven knew how his father thought, and even though he had no doubt his father's plans would change now that Caven worked with Ita, Caven was ready.

They *would* defeat him.

Sebastian kind of wanted the queen to leave, but he wasn't about to tell her that. He suspected that this moment was as important for Caven as rest, and he was willing to give them a few minutes. He wasn't sure what the importance of advisors was, but he could tell it was huge, at least for Caven.

Whatever it was, it made Sebastian like the queen even more. He still wasn't entirely comfortable when they were in the same room, but he supposed that in time, he'd relax. She wasn't just the queen. She was Caven's cousin, his family, just like Christian was for him.

But Sebastian really wanted her to leave.

At least Caven still had a family. His parents had made it public that they didn't consider him their son anymore. He'd sullied their family line by daring to have a child with a human, and they wanted nothing to do with him.

Caven hadn't even been sorry. He'd told Sebastian he didn't care, and Sebastian suspected that was the truth. It shone a light on the kind of relationship Caven had with his parents. It was ironic that Caven would get more power and influence in the clan now that he wasn't talking to his father than before when his father had been scheming in the darkness. Sebastian had no doubt that the asshole wasn't going to stop trying to get to the throne, but at least now, Caven was free.

Besides, Caven hadn't lost much when he'd lost his parents, but he'd gained so much with Sebastian's family. They adored him, and Sebastian had no doubt they were standing outside, waiting to get the news that the egg was out. They mostly seemed bemused by the way pregnancy worked for dragons, but Sebastian was sure they wouldn't care how the child had been born. They'd only care that it was Sebastian's child, and they'd love them as much as they loved him.

Another knock on the door seemed to finally make the queen realize she had better things to do. She said goodbye to Caven and Sebastian and slipped out just as Sebastian's family barged into the room.

"That healer said that you were done," Christian said as he climbed into the nest. "What's his name." He frowned. "Wait, he's a guy, right?"

"What healer are you talking about?" Sebastian asked.

"The hot one, the one who visited Caven several times."

"That's Lisha, and yes, he's male. Why are you asking?"

Christian's cheeks flushed and he looked down at the egg.

170

His expression softened, and he tentatively reached for it. "Can I?" he asked.

Caven nodded and sat in a position that would let Christian touch the egg while allowing Caven to stay wrapped around it. Christian was in awe as he gently stroked his fingers down the length of the egg, and the rest of the family crowded around the nest.

Sebastian climbed out to give Caven and whoever wanted to meet the egg more space. He'd be back there with Caven and their baby soon enough.

Sebastian's father was crying, which almost made Sebastian cry, too. The only one who didn't join Caven and the egg in the nest was Sebastian's grandfather, so Sebastian went to stand next to him. Sebastian's grandfather wrapped an arm around Sebastian's shoulders and squeezed. He was staring into the nest, almost as emotional as Sebastian's father.

"You did good," he murmured.

"I really did, didn't I? Are you happy you're going to be a great-grandfather?"

"I couldn't be happier. And I already am, aren't I?"

"You are, although I'd understand if it didn't feel that way. There's no baby yet."

"There is, and I intend to babysit your child even before they hatch. I don't know how much time I still have left in this world, but I want your child to get to know me as much as possible."

Sebastian didn't want to think about bad things today, so he nodded and leaned against his grandfather. He was surrounded by family, and he could hardly believe that only a few months ago, he was desperate and thought he was about to die.

But Caven had saved him. Patrick was in jail, and he'd stay there for the rest of his life. He would never hurt anyone ever again, which was all Sebastian had wanted. As for the rest—

Caven and their child—he hadn't known he wanted it, but now that he had them, he couldn't imagine life any other way.

About the Author

Catherine is the creator of several series, most of them paranormal, including the Whitedell Pride Series and the Gillham Pack Series. While she graduated in translation, she decided to go the writer's way because it was more fun to create her own stories and characters.

She's been living in Italy for more than twenty years, but she's a daughter of the North—Belgium to be precise—and she misses it so much that she's already planning to move back.

She loves pizza—probably too much—her son, her pets, and of course, books. She sneaks some reading time into her schedule every time she has five minutes free from writing, demands from her various pets and son, and lastly, housework.

Connect with her:

lievens.catherine@gmail.com
BookBub: https://www.bookbub.com/authors/catherine-lievens
Website: https://authorcatherinelievens.com/
Facebook: https://www.facebook.com/catherine.lievens.9
Facebook Group: https://www.facebook.com/groups/411788002341528/
Twitter: https://twitter.com/authorCLievens
Newsletter: http://eepurl.com/c-uvKn

www.ingramcontent.com/pod-product-compliance
Lightning Source LLC
Chambersburg PA
CBHW060820120626
46557CB00001B/294